A LIFE TO WASTE

Published by:

Grand Mal Press

Forestdale, MA

www.grandmalpress.com

Copyright 2016, Andrew Lennon

Library of Congress Cataloging-in-Publication Data

Grand Mal Press/Lennon, Andrew

p. cm

Cover art by Michael Bray

www.grandmalpress.com

THIRD EDITION

For Hazel
Hopefully this is the first of many

ACKNOWLEDGMENTS
Thank you to my wife for the encouragement and help she gave me while writing this

A LIFE TO WASTE

by Andrew Lennon

GRAND MAL PRESS

Chapter 1

What's the plan for tonight then?
    Playstation?
    No, movie?
    No, hmm oh maybe . . . nah, just sleep.

These are the hard decisions that a thirty-five year old, lazy-ass waste of space that lives with his mother has to make.

Meet Dave; average looking, not completely out of shape either, which he should be with his lifestyle. The sort of rough-and-ready looking kind of guy. A bit like Kiefer Sutherland in *Lost Boys* or *Stand by Me*. If he made any effort at all he could probably have his pick of the girls. He makes no effort, none whatsoever. He'll change his clothes, including underwear and socks, maybe once a week, twice on a good day. His hygiene is terrible. His favourite clothes are a big baggy t-shirt and some crumpled jeans, rarely anything different. He doesn't shave until his facial hair irritates him, and even then he just trims it. Dave has a permanent dishevelled look, half tramp and half student.

All in all, he is a scruffy bastard.

He likes to live life at his own pace, any slower and he would be in reverse. His daily routine consists of waking up, eating, playing video games or watching TV, drinking Bud or smoking a doob, depending on his finances—also known as his mother's purse. With such an easy life, well, how could he afford not to? He eats enough for two men, drinks enough for three and let's not get started on the money he spends on weed. It's hard to keep a stable job if you're constantly hung over. That's why Dave decided it would be better all-round if he just didn't work. Why bother? His mother makes enough for them both . . . or so he thinks.

Dave treats his mum like his personal maid. No wait, that's too much of a compliment—maids get more respect. Dave treats his mother like a second class citizen, somewhere between a convict and a leper. To say he has no respect for her is an understatement.

Discarded, dirty clothes, empty plates smeared with crusted food and mould. Dave isn't in the habit of tidying after himself. As you can imagine he doesn't do much cleaning around the house either.

When is mum gets home, she is expected to clean his mess up. If she doesn't he will start insulting her. "Dirty bitch," he will say, "look at the state of your house, how am I supposed to live in *this* shit-hole." His vitriol will continue whilst she cleans, Dave abusing her at any given opportunity. To avoid this ordeal—or lessen it somewhat—it is the very first thing she does when she gets home.

Margaret, Dave's mother, is sixty-five; but she looks older and frailer, closer to seventy-five. Father Time has not been kind to her. Providing and caring for a grown man for twenty years will do that. Dave terrifies her, she lives in fear each and every day. However, she is fit as a fiddle, she can run rings round any woman, or man, at the factory where she works. She can lift boxes twice her weight, which is a constant shock to other workers.

When Margaret has finished cleaning up behind her son, it's time to make dinner. She only prepares very small meals as she cannot afford to eat a lot due to the portions of food that Dave consumes, and the amount of money she outlays. She will cook Dave whatever he desires and save herself a child-size portion of the same food. She *could* afford more food if she refused him money.

She did that once before.

Never again.

He threw an almighty tantrum, like a child in a shop being told that he couldn't have the toy he wanted. Only, a child will kick and scream. Dave wasn't a child, he was a grown man and he didn't kick and scream. He punched and shouted. He didn't punch his mother, although she knew he had come very close and was very capable. Instead, he punched the doors and walls.

Dave is a large man with immense strength, and as a result, there are reminders scattered around the house, physical memories of his anger. Holes in walls and doors, broken furniture etc.

After dinner and the cleaning, if Dave doesn't demand anything further, Margaret will retire to her bedroom for a 'break'. She will read a book or watch the TV. Most nights she lies in bed and wishes something or someone will come and take her away from this endless routine.

Dave hates when his mother is home from work, he prefers the daytime when she isn't there. When she gets home, she will be in his way, picking up clothes or plates or something. It doesn't matter too much though as she is never around for too long. After dinner, she seems to disappear off to bed. He doesn't really know what she does and he doesn't really care. He is fed and the house is tidy, that's all that matters.

● ● ●

There was a *Nightmare on Elm Street* marathon on; this was perfect for Dave. He could sit and drink and smoke and laugh at all the cheesy lines that Freddy Krueger made famous.

The films were terrifying as a child; when Dave and his friend Trevor were younger, they had sneaked the VHS from Trevor's older brother. They went to Trevor's room and watched it. Dave didn't sleep for a week! Every time he closed his eyes, he would see that burned, hideous visage. He didn't dare tell Trevor though, he couldn't let his friend know that it had scared him. He was a tough guy, no way does a twelve year old get scared by silly movies.

As he grew older he thought those films were a little bit cheesy; he was almost embarrassed thinking about how much they had scared him.

Now that he was a drunken stoner, he found these films utterly hilarious. Every cheesy line, or every cheesy killing, he would laugh at the top of his voice. A really loud, horrible laugh which was followed by chesty coughing and spluttering. He'd resolve the noise with another toke, another sip of beer.

Dave was set for the night with this film marathon. There were at least ten films, which could last him the entire night. It would ensure he was sound asleep in the morning so he wouldn't have to speak to his mum before she left for work.

This really was the highlight of Dave's week.

He didn't have friends anymore. He didn't go anywhere, he didn't go to any bars or clubs. He didn't attend sports events or movies. He did join a few social networking sites but he got sick of how happy everyone was. He thought it was all pretentious, people just took happy pictures and posted them online with bullshit statuses; it wasn't their real life. Their real life was sitting in the dark every night watching TV, just like him.

That's what life is like, he thought. *Dark. Everything else is just a lie.*

He wasn't always this horrible lazy loner. He used to be happy, he used to have ambition, and he used to have a girlfriend, Claire. He used to have friends, he had a best friend, Trevor.

Watching the films made Dave think about Trevor, he thought about watching them together when they were younger, back when he was happy, back when life still seemed bright. "What happened to Trevor?" he said to himself. He paused and had another sip of beer. *What happened to me?*

Chapter 2

Dave had been just like any other child; he was happy, popular, he liked to play football, he liked to run—oh boy did he like to run. He could run like the wind blows and none of his friends could get anywhere near him.

When he was nine, he used to race the kids that lived in his area. He even gave them a head start sometimes, but he always won. The only person that was a match for Dave's pace was Trevor; and he was still left for dust.

Quite often, grownups walking past would stop and watch him in astonishment. They had never seen a child run so fast. "You wanna get him on the track," they would tell his parents. "That boy will be running in the Olympics one day."

Obviously his parents didn't think that; they knew he was fast but the *Olympics*? Come on, be serious. Dave believed it, though. "I'm faster than any kid I know," he said, "and my friends said I'm faster than any other kid *they* know." That was when his dream began, his dream of being an Olympic sprinter.

When he started senior school at the age of eleven, things were a lot different for him. Lessons were a lot harder, days were a lot longer, and girls were a lot prettier.

A few things stayed the same though; Trevor was still his best friend, and he still loved to run! He couldn't contain his excitement when he found out the school had an athletics club. He was bouncing up and down, shaking with excitement. "Jesus, calm down before you spurt in your pants," Trevor told him. They were both still waiting for the day when they actually understood what that meant, but they had heard people say it and it sounded funny. "I can't help it," Dave said, "an actual athletics club! Don't you know what this means? This means I can actually compete. I can show people how good I am. This is my ticket to the Olympics."

"Yeah sure, the Olympics." Trevor humoured Dave and carried on walking to class.

Dave joined the athletics team and needless to say, he was the fastest in his year. He noticed, even though he was still winning races, he wasn't winning as easily. The competition got tougher as he got older. This was when he realised that he'd been taking his speed for granted.

With hard work and with training, the other kids could improve and end up being faster than him. So, to stop that happening, he decided to start training himself. Dave went for regular jogs, doing mini sprints at different speeds on different tracks, ones he'd prepared himself. He went to the gym after school, which was free for students.

He kept this routine up for two years, until he reached year nine at school. At thirteen, he could actually compete against other schools, not just his classmates and friends at athletics club. Real competition beckoned. Again, he was overwhelmed with excitement. On the way to his English class, he was telling Trevor how much he was looking forward to racing against stronger opponents. Trevor just nodded and humoured him. He was still friends with Trevor, but with his continuous training, plus homework, which seemed to grow rapidly in year nine, not to mention athletics club, they didn't see much of each other anymore. Outside of school they had different friends. Dave had his running and gym "buddies" and Trevor had his own friends, or "mates" as he called them.

Mates. That's what you called them in school. It was much cooler.

Outside of school, Trevor couldn't be more different from Dave. He and his friends weren't what you would call 'bad kids', but they were not necessarily disciplined either. Trevor and his friends would smoke an unknown amount of cigarettes daily. He would even sell them to the other kids. Twenty pence a cig was the going rate. Other than that, a few of his friends had parents who smoked so they would sneak the odd one out of their boxes. They had to be careful though, they could get away with the odd one easily. If they started pushing their luck they were sure to be caught.

That didn't matter though, they smoked. They were proud of it, it felt cool and grown up. Some of them even went as far as to banter with, "I need to pack in, it's fucking killing me," to which a few of the others laughed. "Yeah sure, you pack in your half fag a day".

On top of smoking, Trevor drank every Friday night.

He didn't care what he drank just as long as it got him drunk. His friends all had the same aim. A Friday night sober was a boring night. They would go through their parents' bottles, taking a little bit out of each. Combined, you could fill a Lucozade bottle. Little bit of vodka, little bit of gin, rum, brandy, whiskey, whatever this green stuff is. Put all that together and you've created a 'shit mix'. No two 'shit mixes' ever tasted the same as they all had completely different amounts and types of alcohol in them. There was one thing for sure though; they all tasted like shit, apt considering the name. But taste didn't matter, the aim was to get you drunk and that is exactly what it did.

Once Trevor and his friends had downed their 'shit mixes', their Friday night adventures could begin. They would set fire to bins outside shops, egg houses in their area. One time, someone suggested egging 'that running kid's house,' but Trevor had managed to talk them out of it. He still liked Dave, even if they lived different lives now.

Finally the day was here.

Dave was going to a regional athletics competition to run against athletes from other schools. He almost skipped to the school bus, then realised just how ridiculous he looked. They were competing against seven other schools from the local area, all of which Dave had heard of.

As Dave was warming up, he watched some of the other events, gauged some of the kids from the other schools. Some of these kids were huge. Granted, many were older than him, the age range of kids competing that day was thirteen to sixteen; Dave was one of the youngest in the group.

There was one kid that reminded Dave of Dwayne Johnson Seriously, sixteen years old and he could give the Rock a run for his money. Dave wasn't worried about him though, apart from being a few years older than him, he was far too big to be a sprinter, and he was probably doing hammer throw or shot put or something.

The competition was a full day event, so there was a lot of waiting round. Dave wasn't racing until 2.15pm. This pleased Dave, it was after lunch, which meant he could stock up on energy, but it was also long enough after lunch that his food would settle and he wouldn't be feeling too full to run. He sat around watching for other kids, other competitions. Besides the freakishly big guys, most of the kids looked the same.

Oh well, he thought, *we'll see them at the start line.*

When it was Dave's turn to race he walked toward the track. He looked at the six other kids he was sprinting against. He was first choice for his school to run the 100 meters—the races were split between first, second and third choice, so he knew that the people he was running against were their schools' first choices. He looked at them again; they didn't look so fast, they certainly didn't look scary, just normal kids.

He walked up to the start line and stood, waiting.

"On your marks."

Dave leaned over, touching his fingers to the ground.

"Get set."

He bent his knees and toes into position, getting ready to spring when he heard the

"BANG"

He was off! He was running faster than he had ever run before, he was sure of it, the wind was blowing against his face, his cheeks and his mouth seemed to be flapping around his face uncontrollably. He thought he must look like one of those astronauts in a G-Force exercise, when he was coming to the finish line he glanced left, he glanced right, he couldn't see anyone, he was sure he had won.

Just as he crossed he noticed that second place finished almost at the same time.

Almost.

"Phew," he sighed, catching his breath, No one had ever come that close to beating him before. He was happy he'd won, but he was even happier at this new feeling he had. He had finally had some real competition, and he had beaten them. But this was just local schools, the competition would be harder in other places, he needed to train more

A few weeks after he had won his first competitive race, he was pulled aside by the teacher that ran the athletics club. "You really have some talent you know, Dave. With some proper training I think you could go really far."

"I do train, all the time," said Dave. "I train my arse off."

"I don't doubt that," the teacher said. "Well, in fact, it's evident by your performance the other week. But when I say proper training, I mean proper athletics training. There is a local athletics club, they train up good young prospects like yourself. Well, one of the coaches there saw you run at that school competition. He wants to know if you want to try out for the club."

"Wow, oh wow, umm hell ye . . . sorry I mean, yes I would love too! Where is it?"

"Well, actually, it's only about a ten minutes' drive from the school. Hell, *you* could probably run there."

So that's exactly what Dave did.

He ran there that day to check it out.

When it came to the day of his try-out, he'd asked his father to give him a lift. Of course, being so proud of Dave, his father didn't hesitate in saying yes. He drove Dave to the local college, where the athletics club was allowed to use their facilities to train. His father hung around and watched while Dave ran different sprints. "Jesus, son, you sure do run fast," Stuart said to himself, "you definitely don't get that from me or your mum." Stuart gave a little chuckle under his breath.

Needless to say, Dave was accepted into the club with no questions asked. "Training will take place on Tuesday and Thursday nights. Your coach will be Phil Davies, so don't be late, he hates it when people are late." His trainer left the room.

The following Tuesday, Dave's father agreed to drive him to training again. In fact he agreed to take him every Tuesday and Thursday to prevent Dave getting injured. When Dave arrived early for training, he met Coach Davies. Or "Phil", as he said to call him. He instantly became Dave's idol. He didn't know this yet, but slowly, Coach Davies would oust Dave's dad as his hero.

Dave's parents, Stuart and Margaret, were a happy couple, they had the perfect marriage, husband and wife, completely in love with each other, and just to top it off, they had the perfect son as well. What more could they ask for?

There was one thing more that Stuart wished for: he wanted to be his son's idol. Maybe it sounded a little selfish or self-centred, but he didn't think so. What's so wrong with wanting his boy to look at him and say, "When I grow up, Dad, I want to be just like you." Dave used to say that when he was younger, he didn't say that anymore. Now all he wanted to do was please Coach Davies. All day, every day it seemed to be the only thing he would talk about. "Phil said

I'm coming on really well," or, "Phil said if I can just push a little harder . . . ''

"Phil said this. *Meh*. Phil said that. *Meh*," Stuart said to himself in a childish little tone. He didn't mean to be jealous but he couldn't help it. After all, you can't control your feelings, and jealousy is one of the strongest.

Dave went to training every Tuesday and Thursday without fail, he never missed one session, he always wanted to please Phil. Every day he would push himself more and more, train harder than the week before. Phil could see the amount of effort he was putting in and accordingly gave him the constant praise that he had earned for these efforts. Phil pushed him to his limit, and sometimes beyond it, in training. When it came to competitions, he tried to pick out the ones he thought would have tougher opponents, be more of a challenge for Dave. Dave still won all the races, but again there were quite a few close shaves.

By the time Dave turned fifteen, the rumour across the country said it all: he was the next big thing. He was going to secure a spot on Team GB without any problems. He was still undefeated in all of his races, which Phil told him was a record. Dave and Phil were more than just runner and coach now, they were practically best friends. Phil really was Dave's hero; after every race his first thought would be, "Phil will be proud of me."

Dave wasn't far off being Phil's hero either, Phil had never seen a boy with such dedication and ambition. He had made him into his own little project, his own little prodigy. He was sure that Dave was going to be the first person he would ever train to compete at the Olympics.

Stuart grew tired of hearing about Phil constantly. Dave seemed to notice this, but he never said anything to him. Stuart never tired of hearing how well Dave was racing, though. His face still gleamed with pride when he watched him cross the finish line, or when he would come home and tell them, "First again". He really couldn't be any more proud.

Plus, Dave was doing well in school. He wasn't the smartest kid in his classes, but he certainly wasn't by any means dumb or falling behind. His teachers said he was guaranteed to get at least B's, but most likely get a few A's as well. He really was the perfect son.

While driving home one day from a competition, Phil and Dave were chatting away. Their usual talk involved strategy for upcoming training and competitions. During this chat, the idea of food came up. It was already past six; Dave had told his mum he would most likely grab some dinner on the way home with Phil. His mum said that it was fine, it was quite a common thing for them to do that, some sort of post-race bonding feed shared by athletes.

Phil was looking in his rear view mirror. "I'm sure I saw something a second ago that looked like a café. I haven't seen an exit yet, though? Maybe I missed it?" He turned round to look out of the back window, to get a better view.

"*Lookout!*" Dave yelled. Phil quickly turned round to see what was coming, but it was too late. The driver's side of the bonnet caught the tail end of a lorry driving in the middle lane. The car spun out of control. Seconds later, they were hit again, hard, by another car that had been driving behind them. After a moment, the obliterated car settled.

The wreck was awful.

The car looked like it had been put through a giant vice and then ripped through a shredder. Dave was trying his best to get out but he was stuck, something was pinning his legs. He shouted, *"Phil! Phil, I can't move my legs!* They're pinned by something, *Phil!"*

But Phil didn't answer. In fact Phil didn't even move. *"Phil!"* Dave shouted again. Still no response, maybe he was unconscious. Dave continued shouting Phil's name while trying to free himself, then just for a second, he stopped. He looked at Coach Davies. He knew instantly then by looking at his face. Phil wasn't knocked out, Phil wasn't unconscious, Phil was dead.

He didn't struggle to free himself anymore, he lay his head back on the chair and cried.

Chapter 3

Dave gave up running after the crash and Phil's death. His coach, his friend. Besides which, he had some pretty extensive muscle damage and a few fractures in his legs from the crash. Even when he had recovered he was never as fast as he had been. His dreams of running in the Olympics had died with his coach. He didn't just give up on running that day, he gave up on life as well. He stopped all his training; with no running what would he be training for?

He didn't put in half as much effort on any of his school work. By the time his exams came round he could only just give enough effort to actually attend, let alone study. He ended up getting mostly D's, a couple of C's and an E. Not terrible results some would say, but he had been told he would easily get B's and if he pushed himself, could count on A's. He used these bad results as another excuse.

Well, there's no point in trying for anything now anyway.

Who is going to give me a job, I'm useless.

He knew that these were just excuses and there was no reason he couldn't go to college or get a job. But he was happy with using these excuses, he had become lazy, he had become complacent and content at the fact that he didn't have to go to college or work.

A positive thing was that Dave was spending a lot more time with his friends now. Since he wasn't spending every minute training or racing, he was left with time to do normal stuff, things that normal kids his age did. He started hanging out with Trevor again and within no time they were back to being best friends. It was like they had never stopped hanging out for the past five years. They went to bars and clubs—they were only seventeen now, but both looked a lot older. Dave had grown to be quite tall and due to his natural frame and years of training, he appeared quite muscular. Underneath the image though, he wasn't half as strong as he was when he was fifteen.

Trevor had long hair down to his shoulders and a beard that could make Chuck Norris look twice. They both looked to be in their early twenties, so getting served was never a problem. Trevor worked Monday to Friday, he was some form of apprentice—in what, Dave didn't care.

So while Trevor worked Dave would sleep, or sit at home playing computer games, waiting for Trevor to finish work. Then they would both meet up and get stoned. They would usually sit outside somewhere to smoke as neither of their parents would allow it in their house. Then, afterwards, they would go into Trevor's to play video games or chill out. They didn't get stoned on a Friday or Saturday, though. Friday night was pub night, Saturday was club night. Trevor could never understand how Dave could afford to keep up with him every week, seeing as Dave didn't work.

Trevor was curious about where he got the money from?

Trevor knew Dave would be getting job seekers allowance, but that wasn't anywhere near as much as they spent each weekend. He just assumed his parents must still be giving him 'pocket money' for helping round the house or something.

Every Saturday when they went to the club, they would try and pull a few girls—they weren't very successful. Dave probably could have pulled every time, but Trevor's appearance—being the long-haired bearded man that he was—seemed to repel the females. There were a couple of times they got lucky, though, managing to convince some University students that they were older than they really were. Overall, this was a rare event.

Dave never expected to meet a girl on a Friday night; Friday night was pub night and they never went on the pull, that was more about getting drunk than looking for girls.

However, he did—it was Friday night when he met Claire.

Dave had never seen Claire before, she had recently moved to the area with her parents. She was a little bit older than Dave, having just turned eighteen, but she looked older, like most girls do. Claire had been having a few drinks in the pub with a couple of her friends, she hadn't really noticed Dave, she had just been happy chatting away. It was her friend, Stacy, who noticed Trevor. Stacy was into the bearded types, and Trevor had reminded her of Dave Grohl.

"Come over and talk to his friend for me while I get to know him," Stacy asked Claire.

"Oh come on, Stacy, I don't wanna be stuck making awkward talk with the *friend*, while you and Charlie Manson go and screw each other." Claire was never shy about sex and things like that.

"It's not going to be like that," Stacy said, "plus, look at his friend, he's cute." Claire turned around to have a look. Stacy was right, he *was* cute.

They both went over to talk to the boys; it took all of

about ten minutes for Stacy to realise that she really wasn't into Trevor. The problem was, it took less than those ten minutes for Claire to fall completely head over heels for Dave. So Stacy was stuck for the night humouring Trevor with small talk. Dave, for the first time in his life, had just gotten his first real girlfriend.

Dave's parents knew that he had a girlfriend, not because Dave told them, he didn't tell them anything. Usually, when they spoke to him the best response they got was a grunt or a mumble. If it was something which actually required an answer then they got a yes or a no. That was it.

Dave had never been the same person after the crash, he had drifted further and further away from them as time went by. They knew that there was pretty much no day in the week Dave was sober. They knew that every day he was either drunk or stoned. They didn't know what to do though; he didn't talk to them or show emotion, so they didn't know how to approach him. They just kept speaking about it between themselves hoping one of them would figure out what to say to him. There was another problem as well. Money was going missing from around the house quite regularly. At first, they thought they were misplacing things, after a while though it happened too often to be coincidence. They couldn't prove Dave was taking it and they didn't want to accuse him. He was already so distant that they didn't want to push him away.

This constant tension started affecting their marriage, they had been arguing quite a lot more and snapping at each other for no reason. They were always apologetic later, they both knew it was just down to stress and were quick to forgive one another. After all, they still loved each other, that hadn't changed, had it?

Or was it strength in the love they shared for Dave that had bound them to each other for so long? This bind was starting to weaken, and although neither of them wanted to admit it, they could feel it. They both started drinking more. It started off as just one drink after dinner, just to settle down and relax. Then it became just a drink after work followed by a drink after dinner. It wasn't long before the drinking lasted from when they got home until they went to bed. This usually led to many drunken conversations and like most drunken conversations, it didn't take long for them to transition into arguments. These arguments became a regular occurrence, three or four times a week.

It wasn't until they were both getting ready to go to bed on one particular Friday that their most bitter argument started.

It hadn't long started when Dave walked through the front door, also drunk. In their intoxicated state, his parents' nervousness and anxiety about approaching him had vanished. The second Dave walked in the door they invited him to join in.

"Oh here he is now," his dad shouted, like he was an announcer on TV. "The fastest boy around. Fucking fastest fingers around more like, ya thieving little *bastard*."

Dave stopped in his tracks, more shocked than anything else; he hadn't really spoken more than a couple of sentences to his parents for the past two years and then he walks straight into this. He hesitated for a moment, but only for a moment, before it was time to say his piece.

All the rage and anger he had suppressed over the past few years, all the hatred he had for himself for how he was letting his life go to waste, all the vitriol he had for some so called deity or fate that had snatched everything away from him. All of those things had been tightly woven inside him like some ever-growing ball of fury.

He released it, he unleashed all those feelings straight in his father's direction.

He roared at his dad; about how he hated him, how he felt he was never there when he had problems, how he looked up to Phil as a father because his dad just wouldn't understand him. All this release was a hell of a lot for Dave—he started to break down.

With tears in his eyes and a lump in his throat, he addressed his father. "You always hated Phil, you hated how close I was to him, and I bet you were happy when he died."

"Now come on, Dave, you know that's not true, I . . . "

Before his dad had a chance to finish his sentence, Dave's tears had dried up. The rage and anger returned. "Who the hell do you think you are, Dad? You're no better than me. All you do is sit round and drink and fight with Mum. What? You like to shout at *her* because she's smaller than you, big tough guy picking on his little helpless wife?"

Dave's mother was staring at his face with sheer terror. She didn't recognise the person that was stood in front of her. A face so angry, so frightening, she wanted to get away from him.

"Well you won't pick on me," Dave screamed.

Her son, the sudden stranger, jumped forward and charged at his father, lunging up and thrusting his hands into his chest. Dave had caught his elder off guard and sent him tumbling to the floor. He quickly jumped on him.

"Dave, son . . . I didn't, I love y—"

His sentence was cut short with a swift punch to the mouth.

"Please, son, don't—"

Another straight dislodged a few teeth, he felt his mouth fill with blood, and he could feel his lips swelling immediately.

"Dave, *don't!*" his mother screamed.

But Dave didn't stop, he lost control, throwing punch after punch, lefts and rights, flying one after another each, reducing his father's face to a crimson, bruised mask.

His mother rushed to him and tried to pull him off, as Dave raised his arm to throw what must've been his fifteenth punch. He drew his elbow back and caught his mother square on the jaw. She fell back onto the floor.

Suddenly, Dave stopped. He turned round to see his mother on her back. He then looked on the floor in front of him and saw the bloody mess beneath him that was his father. He felt complete horror.

"What did . . . I didn't . . . I didn't mean—"

Dave was mumbling. He froze in a complete trance, totally and utterly shocked by what he had just done. He looked around, glancing in a daze back and forth at both his parents lying on the floor, both defeated, both hurt, physically hurt at the hands of their own son. He ran out the door.

Dave spent the entire night walking the streets, he didn't really go anywhere or do anything; he just walked. He spent the entire night thinking about what he had done. How could he do that to his own parents? After everything they had done for him, how could he even think about laying a finger on them, let alone, what he did? He started thinking about how he had lost all his hopes and dreams in that car crash; he lost his coach, he lost his running career, but he hadn't lost his parents. They had still hung in there, every day since, even though he had treated them like dirt, they had never abandoned him. After hours of walking, thinking and being overcome with guilt, he decided it was time to go home. He needed to go and face his parents and apologise.

He knew that his apology wouldn't be enough at first, but he would try, even if it took years, he would try and get them to forgive him.

It was daylight when Dave returned home. He walked into the living room where his mother was sat on the chair crying. He saw that there was blood on the carpet, evidence left from the beating he had given his father. He tried to ignore it.

"Listen, Mum, I'm sorry," he said.

"Well, it doesn't matter now, does it," she replied. "It's too late!"

"What do you mean? Mum, I'm sorry."

"He's gone," she said flatly. "He was unconscious when you left us last night, I thought he was dead." She tried to stop the crying so she could speak, she was able to stop, but still kept losing her breath and sobbing while she spoke. "I spent half an hour just trying to wake him up, you made a total mess of his face. I can't believe you did that. How could you do that to your own *father!*"

Dave wept. "Mum, I didn't mean to, I lost control."

"Well, he's gone now." She said it bluntly. "He said he couldn't live with you anymore. He ignored the drugs, he ignored the thieving, but now he couldn't sit well knowing that any moment you could *kill* him."

"Mum, I would never do that, I honestly didn't mean that last night, I lost control."

"Well, what about next time you lose control, *hey*? You nearly killed him last night. There's no point feeling sorry now, he's gone. He packed his bags and he left."

Dave sat back overwhelmed with what he was hearing. "I can't believe it, I'm so sorry, Mum."

"Well, you bloody should be. It's because of you. What makes it worse is for some stupid reason, I still don't hate you. I want too. I really want to hate you, but I can't and that's my weakness."

She started sobbing again.

"He wanted me to kick you out, or if we couldn't get you out, he wanted to call the police. I said I couldn't do that, I couldn't kick my son out onto the streets no matter what he'd done. I can't forgive you for what you have done, but I can't hate you, for some stupid reason, I still love you and can't see you put out there to waste away. Well, your dad said he couldn't stay here with you. So, he gave me the option, him or you. I chose you."

Dave couldn't believe it; not only had his father left, but his mother had chosen Dave over him.

Why?

After what he'd done, why the hell did she choose for

him to stay? Maybe it was some unwritten rule that a mother has to stand by their kids no matter what they've done or how bad they are. Maybe it was embedded into her brain or her heart. She had let the man she loved walk out the door and it was all Dave's fault. He had never felt so low, so helpless. He'd ruined his family and now there was nothing he could do about it. He leaned over and hugged his mum, gave her a kiss on the cheek and in a soft whisper, with tears in his eyes, he said, "I love you, Mum, I'm sorry I ruined your life." Then he walked slowly to his bedroom and cried himself to sleep.

Chapter 4

Margaret, Dave's mother, didn't know it at the time, but choosing Dave over her husband would become the worst decision of her life.

The morning after the altercation, when Dave had come home and shown remorse, he had been upset and guilty about what he had done.

That didn't last, it didn't take long for Dave to forget about that night.

It seemed like he had forgotten about his father as well, or just didn't care that he wasn't around anymore.

Dave had frequent mood swings; a couple of times a month, he would be so full of anger that he would storm around the house trashing anything in his path. Margaret was terrified of him, she was so scared that when he threw these fits of violence, she would go and hide in her bedroom.

Years had passed now and it was still just Margaret and Dave living together.

They didn't live in the same house anymore, they no longer had their family home, and they had to move to a far smaller house in an area of town plagued with crime. Dave, of course, blamed his mother for this; it was her fault that they couldn't afford to live in their old house. The fact was, she genuinely couldn't afford to keep that house anymore, her sole income wasn't enough to keep up with all the bills and Dave had never bothered getting a job, he left it all to his mother.

The house they lived in now was very small, the living

room was very dark. The reason for this was that only Dave occupied the living room. Margaret always felt tense around him and she couldn't handle the sight of him.

He had ruined her life. Margaret was miserable every single day, she couldn't count the amount of times she had thought about taking her life. She never had any money left after taking care of all the bills, so outside of work she never left the house. She had no friends, no one she could talk to about how her day was or how she was feeling. Sure, Dave was there but it was a waste of time trying to talk to him, he would either ignore her or start insulting her for disturbing him.

Every day she thought about tying her bed sheet around the foot of her bed, then at the other end making a noose and putting it around her neck. Every day she thought about this, then she thought if she just ran and jumped head first out of the window that the sheet would snap her neck. It would be quick, probably painful, but fast. Then it would be over.

But she couldn't do it.

Not because she was afraid of death, she wasn't, she would welcome death right now with open arms if he came knocking. She couldn't take her own life and leave her son alone. She hated herself for still loving him, she wished that she didn't so she could just end it all and leave him to rot in that living room. A mother's love is too strong, even now that she wanted to get rid of it she couldn't; she knew that, somewhere deep down inside, Dave still loved her too.

Maybe that was the hope she was clinging onto.

Maybe one day she would wake up and Dave would

love his mother again, maybe he would be nice and caring again, maybe he would be her loving son again.

Maybe, just maybe.

Chapter 5

It was Friday night, a night when most people like to relax, let their hair down, maybe have a little drink and eat some junk food that tastes just that little bit nicer because they know it's bad for them. Friday night is when the majority of people know that the weekend has arrived and they don't have to face work for another two days.

For Dave, Friday night was just the same as every other night, he treated every night like Friday.

He still ate the junk food, still drank too much and well, relaxed, if that's what you can call it.

What do you call it when someone who does nothing ever, does nothing?

I can't imagine anyone can call it relaxing as they have nothing to relax from. They just continue to do what they always do. I think we can say Dave was vegetating as he was little more than a cabbage anyway. He well and truly lived up to the term 'couch potato'.

Dave had given his mother his orders for tonight. She'd already done the shopping for this week but that didn't matter. Dave had additional orders and there was no chance he was going to go *all* the way to the shop and back. Screw that, his mother could pick up his stuff on her way home from work.

He ordered a box of *Carling*, a large pepperoni pizza, a bag of peanuts, a large bag of tortilla chips and two giant chocolate bars. Dave hoped his order, added to the stash that he already had, would last him the night.

It was just gone midnight and Dave was starting to feel

a little bit tipsy. He only had one or two cans left in his box of lager but he *had* to finish the box before he could go to bed. He had been watching horror films all night again. Tonight had been *Halloween,* followed by *Hellraiser,* and then to finish off he was watching *Candyman.*

Candyman was probably Dave's favourite horror film— all of them were good in his eyes, even the corny ones, but *Candyman* was just that little bit scarier than the others. He didn't quite know why, maybe it was the titular character's voice. Dave loved the scene in the car park when *Candyman* calls out, *"Heeelen, Heeelen . . .Helen."* Every time, that voice would send chills down his spine, he loved it.

As Dave was enjoying the movie in his semi-conscious drunken state, he started to drift off, his head started to droop and gradually his eyes started to close. The can he had in his hand started tilting just slightly, not enough to spill, but getting nearer every second to falling out of his hand. Every minute or so he would jolt awake, sit himself upright again and re-position the can in his hand, then try and carry on with the film.

Once again his eyes would start to close and the can would start to slip. This continued for quite a while and suddenly he jolted awake, but this time was different to the others, this time he had jolted awake to the sound of screaming. He looked at the TV and when gazing at the screen he remembered he had been watching *Candyman.* That explained the screams, so he could settle down and vegetate again. Eyes drooped, can slipped.

The scream was blood-curdling and ear-piercing.

This one made Dave jump out of his intoxicated

dreams so fast that he was stood up off his chair before he even had chance to open his eyes. The can had gone flying out of his hand and he stood in shock, looking left and right and behind him as though whatever it was that screamed would suddenly appear.

He heard shouting again, it was definitely a woman. This time it definitely wasn't on the TV, the film had finished.

"Argh, get off me, you bastard . . . arghhhh . . . "

Dave then realised who it was shouting: it was Lisa from next door.

He sighed, shook his head, walked to the kitchen to grab another beer then plonked himself back down in front of the TV. "Friday night," he said to himself, laughing, then chugged his beer.

The screaming from next door was not a rare occurrence.

Lisa, the woman who lived there, was familiar with what you could call 'complicated relationships'. You couldn't really say that she fought with her boyfriend, because the man she was fighting with changed every time.

To Dave's recollection he had never seen the same man at her house twice. Lisa was not exactly a stunner, she looked a bit like a heroin addict, if truth be told. She was extremely thin, her face was gaunt, he body was emaciated and her hair was long and brown, greasy, it looked like it had never been washed. Dave assumed that based on her looks, the only reason she was able to get so many men was that either she was ridiculously easy game, a slapper, as in she would not say no to *anyone*, no matter how they looked.

Or she was a prostitute.

What amazed Dave even more than Lisa's unbelievable pulling power was that she was able to attract equally violent men every time. It was common that she would bring a guy home and end up fighting with him, physically. It seemed to be literally every single time.

Maybe she was attracted to violent men, maybe she liked it, and maybe she knew which men had a reputation for fighting with women. Maybe she started these fights herself every time, enjoying the drama.

Maybe she would invite a bloke back, perhaps go to bed with him or perhaps not, then at some point decide to give him a good old right hook and see what his reaction was. Maybe it was nothing like this and she was just desperately trying to find love and failing miserably every time. Maybe she was just genuinely unlucky in love.

Dave didn't know exactly what is was. He had many theories, but what he did know—that woman had more fights in her house than Cassius Clay had in the ring. Knowing what he did about Lisa's love life, Dave wrote off the screaming and shouting as being another Friday night fight for her.

Dave didn't feel sorry for Lisa.

Sure, she might be getting a beating every Friday night, but that was her choice, he thought.

She could just stop going home with crazy blokes. Given that he knew just how easy she was, he had been tempted a few times to pop next door and try his chances. He knew she was sure game so it would have been an easy lay. Also, he would probably enjoy going a few rounds in post-sex boxing with her. Yeah she may have looked like the freakish offspring of Snoop Dog and a Twiglet but still, a lay is a lay isn't it?

Other than his mother, Lisa was pretty much the only female that Dave ever saw, seeing as he never left the house. The problem was, Dave had no confidence at all, and he had been overly confident when he was younger but that was years ago, all that had faded away now and left him a shy middle aged loner. By the time Dave was drunk enough to build up enough confidence to even think about going to give Lisa a knock, it was too late.

Fight night had already begun.

Oh well, good for Lisa, at least she was going out and actually getting some action, it was a hell of a lot more than he was getting.

Truth be told, Dave was jealous of Lisa. *Sounds stupid, doesn't it?* he thought.

How could he possibly be jealous of the junkie next door who got a kicking from every bloke she took home on a Friday night? Well, even violence and rage was some sort of emotion, it was something to feel. Yes, it might have appeared horrible to outsiders, but there was no questioning that Lisa felt far more alive than Dave ever did, that was down to violence and rage, the most raw of feelings.

Dave felt nothing from the outside world, it was just him on his own all the time. No emotions, no violence, no anger, no sadness, no love. It wasn't always like that, a long time ago Dave had something really good. He had the love of a good woman, he had someone who would give her life for him at any given moment. He had all the feelings and emotions that he longed for now, he had them poured upon him every day.

It was all gone now though, he had let it all slip away. Some people go through life trying to find love and never succeeding, like Lisa next door. Some people are tormented to go from one person to the next, never feeling that warm feeling inside, never knowing that they are special to a certain someone. Some people are never lucky enough to have any of that.

Dave was lucky enough, he had it all. He didn't know it or appreciate it at the time, but now, approaching middle age, he often looked back at those times.

He once had it all with Claire.

Chapter 6

Claire adored Dave.

Ever since the first night they met in the pub she had wanted to be with him all the time.

He didn't know it then, but Dave loved Claire, he knew that he liked her, he knew he liked her a lot.

Dave and Claire went out together all the time. She was a student and Dave didn't work so they had a lot of spare time. Dave would be quite happy to just sit and drink all day, which is exactly what he did on the days that Claire had her lectures. Claire wasn't a huge fan of drinking, though. Sure, she liked the odd drink. What student doesn't? But she didn't like sitting and drinking all the time, she liked to be out and about doing things, she never wanted to be sat around just waiting for time to pass by.

As a result of this, Claire was always planning adventures for the two of them.

Claire was quite athletic so she didn't have any limitations to what those days would be. Dave wasn't quite as fit as his running days but was still in good enough shape to keep up with her. Besides, he loved to watch her during any strenuous activity.

She was a fair bit shorter than Dave. She always seemed to be tanned; Dave assumed she used the sun beds, but was wrong—she just had naturally dark skin, maybe she had Spanish or Greek heritage in her genes. Claire didn't know for sure but she liked her bronze skin regardless, and so did Dave. She had short brown hair, giving her a tom boy appearance, but her pretty facial features helped her pull it off.

The short hair was chosen, Dave assumed, so that she never had to worry about her hair getting in her way for any of her crazy activities.

Dave was on his way to meet Claire; they were off out again today, he couldn't really remember what they were doing, they did so many different things he could never keep track. Claire always had everything prepared so all he had to do was meet her and they could be on their way. As he turned the corner towards Claire's house he could see her silver Ford parked on the side of the road. Claire was bent over in the boot, pushing things to the back. Dave slowed his walk for a moment so he could have a prolonged look at her shapely rump as she stretched in. He had almost reached her; he was just about to get a cheeky grab as she turned around so his hand quickly slid back to his side.

"Hi, babe," she said cheerfully.

"Hi," Dave replied like a shy school boy.

Claire was always dropping nicknames. Babe. Honey. Sweetie. My gorgeous boyf—that one made him cringe. Dave didn't really do pet names or anything like that, if he was to tell Claire the truth, they kind of annoyed him a little. She liked them though so he left her to it, even if it did embarrass him a bit, especially in front of people.

"So, what are the plans for today then, Claire?" Dave asked. He always called her Claire, seen as that was her name, but he always made a point of saying it, almost as a way to emphasise his dislike of pet names.

"The question you should be asking, darling," she said, sounding like Joanna Lumley. "What do I have planned for this weekend?"

"Weekend!" Dave said, surprised. "But, I haven't even got any clothes, I didn't know that –"

"Well, you did know, because I told you," Claire cut him off. "As I knew that you would forget, because you always forget, I packed for you."

"Oh, ok cool. So where are we going then?"

"We're going camping, babes, with a few activities lined up for while we're there. It's gonna be awesome!"

Dave didn't know what these activities were, but Claire had organised them so he knew they would be quite cool. One thing he did know, though—a weekend camping meant they would be spending nights alone. Together in a tent, now *that* would be awesome.

"Sweet," he said, "so let's go."

"Gimme one second, honey, I'm just gonna grab one or two more things from the house, then we'll be off. You jump in and I'll be back in a mo."

Claire went jogging back up the drive into the house. Dave stood for a second, watching her firm behind as she ran. He really did enjoy that view. Then he climbed in the car and waited for his fun-filled weekend.

The drive seemed to go quite quickly. In fact, it was a couple of hours, but Claire and Dave enjoyed each other's company. Even when they weren't talking to each other time seemed to fly. Eventually they reached their destination; it looked like an abandoned playground or obstacle course of some sort.

There was an empty frame that looked like it had once held swings.

There were long beams of wood placed in various positions around the field propped on other slabs of wood. They were probably used as balance beams.

A climbing wall, which was about six foot high. It was vertically straight on one side a slightly angled on the other.

At the bottom of the straight side there was a pile of tyres, presumably used at some point for kids to climb on so they could reach up to the top of the wall. Now, left in scattered piles, they and the rest of the field gave out a feeling of abandonment.

"Jeebus, Claire, what the hell is this place?" Dave asked

"What's the matter? You scared of a little obstacle course?" Claire replied.

"This doesn't look much like an obstacle course though, Claire, the place is derelict. This wasn't really what we came to do was it?"

Claire laughed. "No, don't be stupid, even if it was still standing, it looks like it's for kids. We're just going to camp here, it's sheltered and we can use some of the wood here for a fire later. It's right next to path that leads up that big hill. I thought we could go on a bit of a trek."

"A trek, hmmm great, I guess," Dave mumbled, looking like a little kid who had to go and visit relatives on Christmas Day.

"Oh, come on, sweetie," Claire said, "it'll be nice to get some clean fresh air. Anyway, it'll hopefully clear some of that shit that you put in your lungs all the time."

Dave looked stumped.

"Come on, babes, you seriously think I don't smell it on you all the time? It's fine as long as you don't do it around me, but make a little effort to mask the smell, hey." Claire smiled.

"Yeah, uh, sorry about that, will do." Dave shuffled, looking embarrassed.

"Come on, darling, it's only a little walk, and besides, later on we can get some real exercise next to the camp fire." She looked at him with a seductive smile. Dave returned the smile.

Dave quite often looked back at that day; it was one of his favourite memories. Of course he enjoyed the 'exercise' by the camp fire, but he surprisingly really enjoyed the walk. The fresh air really did feel nice and he had a lot of time to think while walking through the country hills. Looking back, that was a good day.

But not all days with Claire were that quiet and relaxing.

Most days, Dave actually had to run assault courses. Or participate in activities like white water rafting, paint balling and laser quest. She even had him sky dive once. She was an adrenaline junkie and never wanted to be sat still. Dave loved every minute of it, he always did things on days out with Claire that he would never think of doing himself. When he was out with her he never felt the urge to roll a joint or the need to go and grab a beer. The fun itself was enough influence to keep him happy. When he wasn't with Claire, he made no attempt to go searching for any of these fun things. When she wasn't around the only thing he looked for was drink or drugs.

He didn't see the point in looking for the other stuff, that was their thing, Claire's thing, and drink could occupy him and work just as well until their next adventurous day.

Dave's drinking became more regular. It became a problem.

Claire noticed that he seemed hung over almost every time she saw him. She asked why his drinking had increased. Claire knew that Dave had always been into drinking and smoking weed, but it never interfered with their relationship because he never did it around her. It was like he had more respect for her so wanted to give her his full *sober* attention. Not lately though, lately he had gotten so much worse. When she questioned him he mumbled about problems at home and his dad leaving or something. What he mumbled was quite incoherent and when she asked him to repeat it, he shrugged it off and changed the conversation.

The dates in which Dave was hung over became more and more regular, he never had the energy to go out and do anything that Claire had planned anymore. Instead, they would just sit in and watch a film or do pretty much nothing. This was nice initially, Claire enjoyed the cuddles and snuggling while watching a film. It became too much for her though; this wasn't just once or twice, a nice relaxing date spent cuddling instead of running themselves ragged, it was *all* the time, it bored Claire. She was an active person, she didn't want to be sat on her arse all day watching the world pass her by.

Claire started to nag Dave. "Come on, honey, we haven't done anything fun in ages. We've watched more films in the last month than I had in my whole life."

"I can't be arsed today, Claire, I'm tired and I've got a head ache, maybe next time, okay? Let's just watch the film, yeah." This was the best response that Claire got from that day forward, but she knew that it wouldn't happen 'next time'. She knew that Dave had given up on life and on their relationship.

Claire started going out to do things on her own. *Fine, Dave doesn't want to go, but why should that stop me?* She thought.

It didn't matter what the activity was—climbing, rambling, assault courses, or even surfing—she went and did it all.

Later, she would go and visit Dave and tell him about all the things he'd missed out on.

"Sounds great," was usually the response, then he would focus his attention back into the TV. Claire was hoping that he would like the sound of what she was doing, hoping that he would start to get jealous of her exciting stories and start wanting to go with her again.

It never happened though, he never wanted to do anything.

It didn't take long until she would go to see him and walk into a smoke-filled room where he would be sat with a beer in hand. She hated the smell of smoke, especially from *weed*. He used to save all that shit for when they weren't doing anything together, but now that didn't matter to him.

Claire loved Dave, but she felt hurt every time she went to see him. She knew that he didn't feel the same way anymore, she was sure that once upon a time he did, but whatever had happened, whatever it was that he wasn't telling her, something changed. She knew that it was never going to get any better, and every time she looked in his eyes, there was no response. He had drifted away into some stoned TV land and he had no intention of leaving.

After a couple of weeks of visiting with nothing but drunken or stoned responses to every conversation, she gave up. She didn't see the point in letting herself get upset so often, Dave had obviously stopped caring and she had to try and move on and live her own life, the life she was happy living before he came along. She stopped going round to see Dave and she stopped calling him. She never heard anything from him again and she wondered if he even noticed that she wasn't there anymore, or if he even cared.

Chapter 7

Dave woke up on the couch, hung over as usual.

He sat himself up—falling asleep on the couch, too drunk to make it to bed, was a bit of a habit he had developed over time. He rummaged around the table looking for his smokes, picking up empty boxes then crushing them and dropping them back on the table.

Great, he thought. *Got no smokes and Mum's not back from work for hours. Looks like I'll have to get off my arse and walk to the shop.*

He sat for a while, contemplating whether he could really be bothered to get up, get cleaned, get dressed then walk *all* the way to the shop. "Fuck it," he said to himself, "no one knows me anyway."

He put his shoes on and left the house dressed in the same clothes that he had fallen asleep wearing.

When he walked out the door, the sun hurt his eyes. He wasn't use to natural sunlight much anymore since he rarely left the living room. He squinted and looked around. "What the hell is going on?" he said to himself.

There were police cars and vans everywhere, *and* an ambulance. There was police tape around the narrow walkway into the neighbour's house. Dave remembered hearing Lisa's screaming last night, but he thought that all this was a little bit much. Lisa always had violent times with her many boyfriends but he had never seen anything like this.

The guy must have killed her. This thought rushed into his head. *And I heard her screams . . . and ignored them . . . oh shit.*

He was overwhelmed with an instant feeling of guilt.

Who wouldn't be? He ignored a dying woman's screams. But how was he to know? She screamed all the time, was always fighting. Oh well, maybe he was exaggerating it, maybe it wasn't as bad as he thought. Maybe it was just another fight.

There was a huge police presence there for *something*.

Dave lowered his head and started to walk past the huge crowd that surrounded the police. He kept his eyes glued to the ground trying to avoid any eye contact. This wasn't necessarily because he wanted to avoid the police. He always avoided eye contact, he just wasn't used to people anymore, and he tried to avoid everyone. As he was walking he noticed red marks on the floor and some on one of the hedges as he passed the house.

Is that blood? No, surely not. It can't be.

He quickened his walk and carried on to the shop.

The police and the huge crowd were still there when he returned.

Again, he managed to ignore them and get into his house with no problems. He sat down on the couch and fixed his eyes back on the TV, then he returned to normal Dave mode, vegetation mode. A couple of hours of vegetation mode passed when there was a knock on the door. Dave groaned and decided he would ignore it. Then there was another knock, then another.

"*For God's sake!*" He moaned and slowly got up to answer the door.

When Dave answered the door, he was faced by two police officers. They went through all the formal introductions, then entered the house.

"Did you see or hear anything unusual last night?" Officer Stephens asked.

Officer Stephens looked to be in his forties, Dave didn't know all of the different ranks in the police force, but judging by the way this guy carried himself, and spoke, Dave guessed he was quite high up. You didn't carry that kind of *authority* if you hadn't earned it through years of work. The second officer was a lot younger. Dave thought he had probably just come along so he could observe.

"Didn't really hear anything *unusual,*" Dave said, "I was just sat in watching TV as normal, didn't hear anything . . . apart from Lisa, but . . . " He paused. "But that's nothing unusual, I hear Lisa almost every Friday or Saturday night. You guys must know her well, the amount of fights she has with the dudes she brings home. I'm guessing by all that action this morning that last night's guy really did a number on her, yeah?"

The two police officers looked at each other, then looked back at Dave. Now they had looks of suspicion in their eyes. Office Stephens continued his questioning. "So what exactly do you mean when you say you *heard* Lisa?"

Dave was starting to feel uncomfortable, but he decided he had nothing to worry about, he had done nothing wrong.

Just tell the truth.

"I heard her screaming, I ignored it in all honesty because it's nothing new. There is always screaming and shouting coming from her house. You just . . . get used to it. It's not like I could help her or anything, she would just find another fella to fight tomorrow."

"Lisa is missing," Officer Stephens said bluntly.

This caught Dave off guard.

"Missing?" he said. "How do you know she's actually missing, maybe she just went out somewhere drunk or pissed off after her boxing match last night?"

Officer Stephens replied, "The evidence suggests that there was more than just *a fight* last night. There's a substantial amount of blood, in fact the quantity would suggest that Lisa isn't just missing, she is most likely dead."

Officer Sidekick Trainee chimed in. "Just a bit, the carpet was dripping in blood, and the walls, holy wow, I've never seen any—"

"That's enough. Thank you," Officer Stephens silenced his younger counterpart . "Please excuse my colleague, he is fairly new, but should still know better."

Perhaps they were more than just colleagues, Dave thought, *maybe this kid was his nephew, or even son. That didn't matter, the image this young officer had just put in Dave's head terrified him.*

"What exactly do you think happened?" Dave asked, now looking completely horrified.

"Well, that is exactly what we're trying to find out. Is there anything else you can remember? Anything else that could help us to locate the whereabouts of your neighbour?"

"No, it was just the screaming," Dave answered, but he seemed distant now. The thoughts of this bloody horror show next door had really affected him. "It really wasn't anything different from the norm, honestly, I used to think about going over to help her, but it honestly happens so often now that I assumed she just went looking for it. You can't help people like that."

There was a look in Officer Stephen's eyes. Dave wasn't sure whether or not this man believed him. He was telling the truth though, why wouldn't he? But if the house really was as bad as they said it was, how could it happen without Dave hearing more than just a scream? Maybe there had been more, he was pretty drunk, he could have slept through it. He had those horror films on too, maybe he could have mistaken Lisa's screams for something on the film. It could be done, couldn't it? Especially when drunk. He thought about saying this to the police but he stopped. Would it start to sound like he was making excuses? He didn't want to start making himself sound guilty. He didn't want to start drawing unnecessary attention to himself.

"Do you really think she's dead?" Dave asked.

"Like I said, we are trying to find out exactly what happened. We will be questioning other people in the area as well as you. I would imagine that we will have a few more questions at a later date. Will you be here if we need to contact you?"

"Yeah, I'm always here, I don't do anything." Dave said. "I mean, I don't *work* or anything, so yeah I'll be here if you need to get in touch with me. Mum will be back later as well, she's at work right now."

Officer Stephens and Officer Sidekick Trainee thanked Dave for his time and made their exit. Dave returned to the couch. This time he wasn't as engrossed in the TV as normal. This time he was engrossed in his thoughts.

What the hell happened to Lisa? What was that guy talking about with all the blood? Exactly how much blood was there? Could it have been an animal? Could it have been one of the violent guys she likes to bring home? What happened? Is she, is she really dead?

All these thoughts came one after another, flooding Dave's mind with terror, then worse thoughts came.

What if it was a serial killer? What if he came to my house instead of Lisa's? What if he comes back?

Dave tried to block these thoughts out but it didn't work. They kept flooding back into his mind. He carried on creating horrible bloody images in his head. How the hell could he stop these thoughts?

"Beer," he said, "I need beer."

Usually, he would have contacted his mother to tell her to grab some for him on the way home.

Not this time though, he couldn't wait till later, he needed beer now.

So, for the first time in years, for the first time since before the crash, he ran.

He ran as fast as he could.

He ran all the way to the shop. He grabbed a crate of twenty-four cans of Stella. He usually drank Carling, but Stella was stronger and he felt that he needed to get completely wasted to remove these thoughts from his mind.

He didn't usually drink spirits but he grabbed a bottle of whiskey as well, just in case. He had stolen fifty quid from his mum's drawer before he left, so he even had a bit of change to grab some more smokes as well.

Then, with booze and smokes in hand, he ran again.

Granted, not very fast this time being loaded up with all those cans and a whiskey bottle. But he ran anyway, ran all the way back home, shoved a load of cans in the fridge, opened one and downed it before even moving from the spot.

He grabbed another and returned to the couch.

Oh yeah, he was getting shit-faced tonight.

That would purge these thoughts from his mind.

He hoped.

Chapter 8

Dave was sat in front of TV, again.

He wasn't even sure what he was watching, he was more *looking* at the TV than actually *watching* it. He heard a noise come from somewhere else in the house, he couldn't quite place where.

He shouted, "Mum? Was that you? What you broke this time?" Under his breath, he mumbled, "Clumsy bitch."

There was no answer, but then he didn't want or expect an answer, he was just shouting so his mother knew that he had heard her break something.

BANG.

"What the fuck?" Dave uttered.

This wasn't just something being dropped, what was that?

"Mum! What the hell was that?"

Again, no answer.

"*Mum!*"

No answer.

"Urgh," Dave groaned and got up. "Fine I'll go see what's up! You best not have broken anything, Mum, or I swear to God!"

He walked into the kitchen and had a look around. There was no one there, nothing wrong, everything looked fine. He went to the bathroom, again no one there and nothing wrong. He checked his room and then finally his mother's bedroom, no one there. She wasn't in.

"What the hell was all that noise then? Hearing things now, Dave?" He said to himself. "And now talking to yourself as well, losing your bloody mind."

Dave walked back to the living room and plonked himself back on the couch.

BANG.

"Seriously, what the hell is that?"

He knew he had already checked everywhere and he knew he was the only person in the house. Still, he felt that he had to go and check everywhere again. He walked around all the rooms again, checking for anyone or any sign of something that could have made that noise.

Again, nothing.

He walked back to the living room. He started to feel like he was being watched. He carried on turning around to look behind him, and he felt chills going down his spine. He was being watched, he was sure of it. He turned to look behind him again, nothing. He sat back on the couch.

BANG

"Again?"

He turned around, this time there was something behind him.

"Oh, shit! What the fuck?"

There was a huge shadow behind the couch.

Dave jumped up and turned around so he was stood facing the shadow, but there was no one else there.

It wasn't his shadow.

Was it a ghost?

He was terrified. The shadow flinched. Dave jumped in fright. The shadow began moving to the left side of the wall. Dave, paralysed with fear, stood staring at the shadow. To the right, he noticed movement. Another shadow had appeared on the right hand side of the wall. He looked behind him, no one there. Where were these shadows coming from? Who did they belong too? Dave's fear was growing inside him, he felt himself shaking, he could feel sweat dripping down his forehead.

Are these things monsters?

Are they here to kill him?

The two monsters stood stationary on the left and right sides of the wall. Dave froze, almost like he was in a standoff with these two *creatures*. He noticed something else, something starting to fall from the ceiling. It began to move down the wall.

This wasn't another shadow, it was something else, some form of liquid. It was red. It was thick. It was blood.

"Oh shit, oh shit, what the fuck is going on?" Dave said, his voice high pitched, almost sounding like a small child.

The shadows still didn't move, just stood still staring at him. He couldn't see that they had any eyes but he knew that they did. He knew that they were watching him, staring through the black pits that were hidden in the huge black hole that shaped their body.

The blood continued to spill from the ceiling down the wall, it had reached the floor now, a puddle was starting to form at the bottom of the wall.

This is what happened next door, Dave thought, *this is what happened, these things came and took Lisa and now they've come for me.*

The puddle continued to grow, the blood started to creep along the floor towards Dave. He stepped backward, trying to distance himself from it. He kept stepping back until he reached the wall. The blood kept coming, splitting into different routes, looking like fingers from a growing hand reaching out for him, it kept coming. The shadows started moving in, closing in on the room, they weren't just covering one wall now, they were surrounded the whole room. Darkness was growing all around Dave. The only thing he could see were the black giants surrounding him and the red blood hand reaching for him across the floor. They were coming to take him.

He screamed, "*Nooooo!*"

Dave sat up.

He was still on the couch. He had fallen asleep, drunk again. The TV was still on, he looked around. There were empty Stella cans all over the floor and an empty whiskey bottle next to him on the couch, which presumably Dave had been sleeping on.

It had been a dream, well a nightmare.

"Thank God," Dave said, sighing in relief.

He was pretty shaken up, it must have been all the thoughts about Lisa next door playing on his mind. Drinking to forget about the scenes next door didn't work as well as he had planned. In fact it looked like it made it a hell of a lot worse.

That was only the first nightmare. The next night he had a second nightmare.

Then the next night, then the next.

It came to the point that he was getting too scared to sleep. Lisa's body still hadn't turned up, which meant whoever or whatever had been the cause of the house next door being covered in blood still hadn't been found.

This didn't help with Dave's dreams. *What if it came*

back? What if his dreams actually came true?

They felt real enough to him, he was overwhelmed with fear. He tried staying awake, he started drinking coffee when he felt tired. It didn't work, he still fell asleep, even during short naps, just closing his eyes for a couple of minutes. The dreams came rushing back into his mind and he would wake up screaming again. The lack of sleep was starting to make him feel ill.

He decided that enough was enough.

Regardless of what had happened next door, he was a grown man and he couldn't be making himself sick through fear of sleep. He decided he would go to the doctors and see if there was something they could give him. Something which could help him sleep throughout the night without waking every ten minutes. He had heard that sometimes if you took sleeping pills that you could sleep without dreaming at all. He had also heard that sometimes they could amplify the dreams. It didn't matter, his dreams couldn't get any worse than they already were.

He had to do something.

He called the doctors to book an appointment.

Chapter 9

"Take a seat," Doctor Spring said. "So what seems to be the problem?"

Dave shuffled in his chair. He was looking everywhere in the room, at his feet, at the pictures on the walls, at the doctors computer. He looked everywhere except at Doctor Spring. He would make quick glances towards the doctor's face, but he would quickly look away when accidental eye contact was made. He was biting his nails, then messing with his hair, then he would go back to biting his nails while frantically looking everywhere in the room again.

He was a complete mess, sleep deprivation had really started to take its toll on him.

"Well, you see, the thing is, I . . . erm . . . "

Dave's voice was quick and jittery, it almost sounded like he was on speed or ecstasy.

"The thing is . . . erm . . . I'm struggling to sleep, I . . . I need some, you know, some sleeping pills, you know so I can sleep."

Doctor Spring sat back and looked at Dave. His initial thoughts were that Dave *had* been taking some form of drugs; all Dave's mannerisms seemed to suggest that. But his pupils were not dilated, and although he was jittery, he didn't show any other signs of drug addiction, besides the nervousness. The doctor suspected that maybe Dave liked to drink a lot and added to this sleep deprivation were symptoms of alcohol withdrawal.

"Can I ask, have you been taking any recreational drugs?"

"No," Dave answered without hesitation.

The only drug he had now-a-days was weed and he hadn't smoked anything in over a week. He hadn't touched any drink either, though he had thought about it. He thought that booze and weed might have helped him sleep but he felt too ill to touch either. He had been feeling too ill from the lack of sleep.

"Ok, and how much do you drink?"

"Not much, just a few cans every other night," Dave lied.

He knew where this was leading and he didn't want to be signed up to some alcoholic twelve step programme, he just wanted something to help him sleep. If he wanted to deal with any alcohol or drug problems he would do that in his own time when he wasn't so tired.

"Listen, Doc, the thing is, I erm . . . the problem is . . . I've been having these dreams."

Dave proceeded in his jittery nervous voice to explain his dreams to the doctor. He told him about the police coming to the house, he told him that there was a murder investigation ongoing in relation to his next door neighbour. He told him how he was too scared to sleep and the longer it went on the worse it got. The very brief spells of sleep he did have were filled with even worse nightmares because he had built them up himself by trying not to sleep. It was a vicious cycle and he couldn't see any way of stopping it.

"So you see, doc, that's . . . that's why I need those, erm, those sleeping pills, so I can have a kip and . . . I can start getting over all these crazy thoughts and nightmares. I just need erm . . . just one full night's sleep. You know, even with nightmares, at least if it . . . you know more than ten minutes, that'll fix me right up you know?"

Doctor Spring could see that Dave was genuinely desperate to sleep. He had read in the paper about the investigation for the missing local girl so he knew that Dave wasn't making the story up. He gave Dave a lecture as to how these sleeping pills are addictive and usually not recommended. In the end he decided to give Dave a prescription for the pills. He explained that he would only issue one week's worth of pills due to the risk of addiction.

"So let's see how you do with them, any problems then come back and see me."

"I . . . I will do," Dave said, genuinely thankful. "Thanks, thank you!"

Dave grabbed his prescription from the chemist inside the doctor's office then went straight home. He washed two pills down with a glass of water and went to lie on his bed.

Oh God, I hope these work, he thought. *I hope they don't make these dreams worse though, oh actually I don't even care about them anymore, I just hope they make me sleep.*

After half an hour of these repeated thoughts, Dave fell asleep.

Chapter 10

"Go on, Dave, you can do it," Phil shouted.

Dave looked over to see his coach cheering him on, he looked at the runners either side of him. They looked nervous.

"On your marks."

Dave walked to his starting point, shot the crowd a quick glance and noticed his parents. He couldn't hear what they were saying, he tried reading their lips, but he still couldn't make it out. Maybe they were wishing him luck. He didn't need luck, he had this in the bag, he had been training harder for this race than anyone else.

This was the big one, the one that Phil said would set him up for life, the one all the big scouts were watching—he just needed to win this race. He recognised a couple of the guys he was racing having raced them earlier in the year. Before, he'd destroyed them. He knew they didn't stand a chance, especially with all the additional training that he had been doing.

"Get set."

He crouched down, waiting for his moment, waiting for that all important gunshot, that one moment that would set him free. He was ready, he knew the second he heard it that he would be sprinting down that track faster than he ever had before, and he was going to be running like *The Flash*. He imagined people getting whiplash by watching him and chuckled to himself.

This was the moment he had been waiting for, for so long.

His time, this would be the point that all the training would pay off.

The defining moment.

BANG.

He was off. Dave was sprinting down the track like a cheetah chasing its prey. He was running faster than he had ever run in his life. He knew there was no chance anyone was catching him. His feet pounded the ground, his thighs felt ready to explode.

This is it, he thought, *I'm winning! I'm going to win, I'm going to the Olympics.*

As he was hurtling down the track, Dave glanced at the crowd. Coach Phil was standing next to his parents, they looked like they were moving in slow motion, all three of them looked the happiest they had ever been. Phil's face was shining, he had a smile from ear to ear. Dave's parents were hugging each other and jumping up and down with joy.

"Go on, son! You're winning. *You're doing it!*"

Dave looked straight ahead to the fast approaching finish line. Claire was standing at the finish line calling his name.

"Come on Dave. Nearly there. You're going to win. *Go, Dave, go.*"

He started to pick up his speed, shifting gears, and he could feel the wind blowing against his face, his cheeks flapping like an astronaut feeling the G-Force from a rocket launch. He was the fastest man alive, he was sprinting his way into the record books. Fame beckoned.

He crossed the finish line and ran straight into Claire's arms. He picked her up and cheered for joy.

"I did it! I won."

He rubbed his nose against hers, he tilted his head to the side to kiss her.

He woke up.

"Urgh, what?" Dave sat up confused. "It was a dream?" He sighed.

He looked around the room, he could see daylight sprinkling through the window. He'd slept all through the night.

Brilliant. Those sleeping pills worked a treat, he thought, *I feel bloody brilliant after that sleep.*

Dave hopped out of bed and walked to the bedroom door. For the first time in as long as he could remember, he'd woken up happy. He walked with a spring in his step, he was on the verge of skipping he felt so good.

He opened his bedroom door and his jaw dropped.

His face twisted in shock, he looked down to see that he was standing in a river of blood. He looked back up, the room was red, and the walls were soaked with blood.

He screamed.

"*Mum!*"

Chapter 11

Dave ran through the house looking for his mother.

He could feel his feet squelching in the cooled blood that had soaked into the carpet.

Everywhere he looked he could see all shades of crimson, it was smeared over the walls, all over the furniture and all over the woodwork.

What the hell happened, how could he have slept through all this?

The place was trashed, how could he not hear a thing last night?

He ran to his mother's room, it was empty. All that remained was the aftermath of what ever happened last night. Her TV was on the floor, broken. What little personal items she owned were scattered around the room. Her bed was dark red, it had what looked to be a puddle of blood in the middle of it, so much that the bed and sunken a little in the centre.

Dave left his mother's room to check everywhere else in the house. She was nowhere to be seen. Whatever or whoever had made all this mess had taken her with it. Or what was left of her, how could she even still be alive in she had lost so much blood? Dave dropped to his knees, struggling to breath in a state of shock and fear. He was shaking, he vomited on the floor.

Then, he began to cry.

A couple of hours passed. Dave was taken from the house to the police station. They had checked him out in the back of an ambulance to make sure that he had no wounds. He explained that nothing happened to him, he woke up and it was already over. Whatever took his mum didn't touch him. Regardless of Dave's explanation, the paramedics checked him over anyway.

"Hello again, Dave." Officer Stephens uttered as he sat down.

Officer Sidekick Trainee was nowhere to be seen. Stephens had a new partner who didn't introduce himself or say anything, he just sat there, watching. Dave chose to ignore him, he assumed that this guy just *had* to be there for some legal reason or something like that.

"Hi," Dave mumbled.

"So, how are you feeling?" Officer Stephens asked.

"I've been better," Dave answered.

"Yeah, I'll bet." This almost sounded sarcastic to Dave. "So," Officer Stephens continued, "would you care to tell me what happened last night?"

"I . . . I don't know," Dave said, his voice quivering as he spoke.

"Come on, Dave, how could you not know, you were there weren't you? The house can't end up like that without you noticing!"

"No, I was asleep."

"Asleep? You expect me to believe that you slept right through while someone trashed your house and did *whatever* they did in there last night. The place was an abattoir!"

"*Yes,*" Dave shouted back. "I hadn't slept in weeks. I took some sleeping pills last night, I slept right through till morning, and I didn't hear a bloody thing."

"Right, ok, so let's say you *did* sleep right through from

these sleeping pills, where did you get them from might I ask?"

"I got them from the doctor. I haven't been able to sleep since . . . you know . . . what happened to Lisa, so the doctor gave me pills."

Officer Stephens jumped at this. "No. We still don't know *what* happened to Lisa do we? All we know is that now your mother is off to join her, wherever she has run off to. And the only person who seems to know anything is you, Dave."

"No, I don't, I didn't hear anything—"

"—this time. You didn't hear anything *this* time." Officer Stephens interrupted "You heard the screaming the first time, remember?"

"Yes, I mean, I didn't hear anything this time. The sleeping pills must have knocked me out." Dave knew this guy didn't believe him, he knew that he was going to be the number one suspect for his mother's murder.

The questioning carried on for a long time and Dave didn't have much to answer as he genuinely had slept through what ever had happened last night. A few of the questions got repeated almost as though the police were trying to catch him out, to see if his answer this time was different from the last. Unfortunately, Dave couldn't be any help at all to the police. His answers never changed, they were a compilation of 'I don't know' and 'I'm not sure'. Then he was left with the old clichés of 'ok, we'll be in touch soon for more questioning' and 'make sure to don't go anywhere as we will want to get hold of you.'

Dave had no intention of going anywhere, he had

nowhere to go and he had no friends or relatives that he knew of, besides his dad who it hadn't seen in years.

Dave was put up in a hotel room for a couple of days. He couldn't stay at the house since it was now a crime scene. Aside from what it could do to his mental state, the CSI team needed access while they collected vital evidence. He received a few more visits from Officer Stephens to ask him more questions. They were pretty much the same things he had already been asked prior to these visits, his answer was still the same.

"I don't know."

Apparently, a 'cleaner' had been appointed by the police. This guy's job was to go and safely clear up all the blood and mess that was left in the house so it would be suitable for Dave to move back in. Dave had seen a film about this named *Cleaner*. It had starred Samuel L Jackson as the titular character. This had made Dave chuckle, he imagined Jackson at his house cleaning up, how cool would that be? His laughter quickly faded when he thought about exactly what it was that he would be cleaning. On the film, they use Listerine to help clean as it acted as a de-coagulant to the blood.

He wondered if this was actually true.

Officer Stephens paid another visit to Dave; the CSI team had gathered all the evidence they needed. There was something strange though, an irregularity. Something they needed to check with Dave.

"So, where do you think all that blood came from?" Officer Stephens asked.

"What?" Dave asked, shocked. *That bastard. How the hell*

could he ask him that? He knew damn well where that blood came from. It had come from his dying mother. What kind of sick prick would ask someone a question like that?

"Are you fucking kidding me?" Dave looked up in astonishment.

"Okay, Dave, I can tell from your reaction that you definitely knew nothing about this. I may as well put your mind at ease, a little bit at least." Officer Stephens straightened his posture and raised his head as if to deliver some ground breaking discovery. "We think your mother may still be alive."

At first, Dave said nothing. A moment passed. "Really?" Dave finally asked. A feeling of joy rushed through him and his face broke out into a huge smile. "Have, have you found her?"

"No, I said we think she *may* be alive, Dave, we haven't found her, not yet."

"Then what do you mean?" Dave felt crushed once again. *Was this prick just playing with his emotions now?*

"The blood in your home did not belong to your mother, Dave. It was pig blood, we didn't find anything else other than pig blood."

Dave was baffled. "What the hell? Why would someone come into my house and decorate it in pig blood? Where the hell is my mum then?"

"We're not sure, yet, we do suspect that whoever took her is the same person that took Lisa."

Dave sat back overwhelmed with this news, a rise of emotion bubbled in his stomach. He was more confused than anything else. Was his mother alive or not?

Officer Stephens went on to explain that the most likely reason for the pig blood was to make it look like the victims had, in fact, been murdered in their homes and then the bodies removed. Perhaps whoever had done this wasn't very intelligent and they didn't know about the capabilities of police investigation teams and scientists nowadays. Maybe they didn't know that these teams would be able to tell where the blood had come from almost immediately. Or maybe they had done this to shock people. Maybe they were one of those crazed attention seeking criminals and wanted their story plastered all over the paper.

None of this mattered, what mattered was there was a chance that Dave's mother was alive and the police were going to find her.

Dave was told that his house had been cleaned now. He could return home when he liked.

He returned the next day, but he was under strict instruction from Officer Stephens not to stray too far away; he was still a suspect and he had to be readily contactable for more questions at any time. Dave had no intention of going anywhere, his mother was alive.

The only thing he had to go on was that whoever had taken Lisa had come back to take his mother, so there was a chance, hopefully a big chance, that they would come back for their next victim. Dave just had to make sure he was around when they did.

He didn't bother to tidy any of the mess that remained. The furniture had been thrown around but besides that the place didn't look too much different from before. The blood was gone and that's all Dave was concerned about.

Okay, now he just had to wait.

When this sick psycho came back Dave would be wait-ing for him.

He was going to find his mother.

Chapter 12

No more sleeping pills.

That was Dave's first decision. If this person or *thing* came back, he wanted to be ready for it.

It had been to his neighbour's house and then his, he was sure that it would come back to another house close by. If he was awake every night, stayed really quiet and kept a look out, he would be able to catch this thing . . . person.

He decided to stock up on coffee, energy drinks, milk and cereal. The stimulants could keep him awake through the night, the cereal and milk gave him food whenever needed. He didn't need to leave his post (a chair by the window) to have to go and cook food. Cereal was quick and easy.

Coincidently, it was also cheap and with his mother missing, Dave didn't have much money.

With his supplies at the ready, he spent his first night sitting up, waiting. It was a really long night. Dave had underestimated just how difficult it would be to sit in silence waiting for the whole night. He had gone through a ridiculous amount of coffee, at least ten cups, and he had gone through three energy drinks. Still, he felt like he was going to fall asleep.

By 3am he did.

This wasn't going to work. He needed to change his approach.

He decided to sleep through the day, he knew that this thing wasn't going to come and take people while it was still daylight. So, he allocated himself the hours between 10am and 7pm to sleep. That gave him a good six to nine hours sleep depending on how easily he nodded off. Then he would be set to sit up for the night, he wouldn't be anywhere near as tired.

It still wouldn't be enough though, he needed something to hold his attention. He couldn't have the TV on, apart from the fact that it would distract him from his 'guard duty', the noise from it might make him miss anything that was going on outside.

Books were the answer—he could sit in silence reading a book, it would hold his attention more than staring into the empty night and he could get them for free from the library. He knew where the library was but he had never been in there. Who knows, he might even learn something from reading a little bit as well. He stepped through the door.

"Hello, can I help you?" The cheerful librarian asked.

"Hi, yeah . . . um . . . I'd like to join the library," Dave asked nervously, sounding like a fifteen year old asking for cigarettes at a shop counter.

"OK, just fill this in please."

The librarian gave Dave a laminated sheet of A4 paper and a felt tip marker. The form asked for all the usual information. Name, address, age, date of birth. Dave filled in the form and handed it back. The librarian quickly entered his info onto the computer, grabbed a library card and wrote his name on the back of it. She scanned the barcode, which was followed by a beep from the computer then handed the card to Dave.

"Ok, you're all set," she said.

"Thanks," Dave said. He noticed her wiping his details

off the laminated form as he walked towards the book-shelves.

Saving the planet, I guess, he thought to himself.

Dave had never been much of a reader before so he wasn't entirely sure what he was looking for. He guessed that if he chose books that were similar to his taste in films, he couldn't go far wrong. Horror was his favourite film genre so he decided that's what he would go for with books. The horror section in the library was a lot smaller than all the other sections.

Maybe horror isn't quite as popular as the other stuff, he thought, *maybe there were some horror books in the thriller or Sci Fi section?*

It didn't really matter, there were still enough books in the horror section, there must be *something* to read. He scanned the books for a while then decided it would be safest to go for authors he had actually heard of. He chose *Charlotte* by Stuart Keane, *Amnesia* by Matt Hickman and *IT* by Stephen King.

This should be more than enough, he thought, although he was pretty sure that he probably wouldn't get much further than *IT*. It looked like a mammoth of a book and it would probably take him a month to read. He had loved the movie though so decided this was definitely the book for him.

Dave was all set, he had slept solid from around 11am right through until 6.30pm, which had given him seven and half hours sleep. He drank an energy drink, followed by a cup of coffee, and sat himself down with his bowl of ce-real and *IT*. Now, he knew he was going to be able to stay awake, so he could wait and be ready for this thing whenever it turned up.

Then a terrifying thought entered his mind.

What exactly was he going to do when it did?

Chapter 13

Three days of Dave's 'night duty' had passed. He kept to his schedule as planned, sleeping during the day so he had the energy to stay awake through the night. He had heard and seen nothing so far. Each night he sat in silence in a barely lit room. The only light was the lamp he placed on the table next to him so he could see his book. Outside was dark, there had been no movement apart from the odd car driving past or one of the teenagers that lived somewhere down the street stumbling past at early hours in the morning.

Dave started to wonder if he was wasting his time; was this thing really going to come back to the same spot *three times?*

Would it be that cocky, or stupid?

It didn't matter, he had to keep hoping, this thing *had* to come back, and it was the only way that he would be able to find his mother.

After a toilet break, Dave returned to his table and opened up his book. He was a couple of hundred pages into it now, he had been struggling a little bit as a novice reader, but overall he was following the plot quite well and was enjoying it.

It was another really quiet night, so quiet that it started to make Dave feel on edge. *There's something eerie about complete silence,* Dave thought, *noise is comforting.* Dave would be a lot happier if he lived on a busier road where there was a constant flow of traffic, the silence was starting to get to him.

He heard a noise.

What was that? he thought to himself, then sat almost as

if he were waiting for an answer.

Another noise.

There it is again.

The sound of scurrying footsteps came from one of the other rooms.

"Oh, shit someone's in the house," Dave whispered to himself. "Who's there?" he shouted, trying to hide the fear in his voice. He heard the scurrying again, it sounded like children running around in one of the bedrooms. "I said who's there?" This time with more authority.

The running stopped. Dave walked very slowly across the room, he reached around the door and turned the light on to the next room before entering.

There was no one there.

He checked his bedroom, his mum's bedroom, the kitchen, the bathroom. All empty.

Unless they were hiding? He stood for a second taking deep breaths, trying to build up the courage to go and look. He checked his mother's room first, checking the cupboards, behind the door and under the bed, all the usual places he could think of. Then, he checked the bathroom, aside from behind the shower curtain there was nowhere to hide in there. Empty. That left his bedroom. Dave checked his cupboard, also empty. That only left one place—under his bed. He heard giggling.

"Oh, *shit*," he shouted, louder than he meant to. "Ok, you bastard, get out from there before I kick your arse!"

He heard the giggling again.

Dave felt his stomach tighten, he felt like he was going to puke, he was absolutely terrified. *Who the hell was this hid-*

ing under his bed? It sounded like a child, and he couldn't be scared of a child, could he? Where did the child come from? Why were they here? What if it wasn't a child, what if it was the thing that took his mother?

"Okay, *that's it*," he shouted

He grabbed the side of the bed and in one swift motion lifted it on one side and threw it upwards. It rolled over and landed upside down a couple of feet away.

"What the . . . but, I heard . . . "

There was no one there, he must have been hearing things. All this sitting alone in the dark, in silence all night must have been playing with his mind.

It sounded so real, he thought to himself.

Dave walked back to his chair, sighed and sat back down with his book.

There was the giggling again, followed by hurried footsteps running from room to room.

"Right, that's it!"

Dave jumped up and sprinted to his room, this time filled with more courage. He was tired of being messed with. "Come on out, you bastard. *Come out!*" He ran round the house from room to room screaming like a mad man, throwing things around, tearing open cupboard doors so hard that the wood splintered. There was still no one there. Eventually he stopped, leaning over to catch his breath.

"Shit, Dave, you've lost your fucking mind," he said to himself puffing for air.

Another try, he sat down and opened his book. He started to question whether his choice of book was a good idea. What it really his best plan to sit alone in the dark all night in complete silence and read a horror story? So what, it was just a story, it wasn't like a killer clown was going to jump out and get him, he hoped.

No don't be stupid, whoever it was he waited for would just be a human being.

Perhaps a sick deranged human being, but still, there would be no killer clowns chasing him around the house.

He opened his page and started to read again.

He heard something else.

"Oh, you've got to be fucking kidding me, what now?"

This wasn't coming from inside the house, this sounded like it was coming from outside. It was music.

"What the hell is that?" he whispered.

The music was faint, very slow. It sounded like a jack in the box being turned slowly. Almost as if whoever was turning it was trying to build tension, waiting for the precise moment to make the scary clown jump out and terrify whoever was watching it. Just one beat at a time, it was a painfully slow tune. He recognised it though, each beat followed by what seemed to be an eternity before the next one came.

It was *Teddy Bears Picnic*. He said the words to himself slowly, in time with the tune being played.

"If. . .you. . .go. . .down. . .to. . .the. . .woods. . .today." It sent shivers down his spine; it was the creepiest thing he'd ever heard. It was definitely coming from outside.

What the hell was that?

"You're . . . sure . . . of . . . a . . . big . . . surprise."

He peeked out the window.

Chapter 14

Dave's jaw dropped. "It can't be," he said.

He looked at his watch to double check the time, which read 2.30am; the middle of the night. He looked out of the window again. Outside there, in the darkness, stopped at the side of the road, was an Ice cream truck.

Why the hell would an ice cream truck be out there at this time of night?

"It's happened, I've finally lost my mind," he said to himself.

The music carried on, it's steady slow pace, he couldn't help but sing it again in his head. "If . . . you . . . go. . .down . . . to . . . the . . . woods . . . today."

This couldn't be real, he had to be hallucinating or something. Maybe his sleeping-during-the-day theory wasn't really working. Maybe he had drunk too many energy drinks or perhaps this was the book playing on his mind again. It could be that he was just seeing things, and the music was just in his head. Like the giggling children before. This wasn't real, this was just in his head. He looked outside again. It was still there, music still playing.

"You . . . better . . . believe . . . your . . . eyes."

No way, this couldn't be real.

He decided to go outside and prove it to himself. He grabbed his coat and put his shoes on. He knew that when he walked outside he would see that there was no ice cream truck. He would see that it had just been his mind playing tricks on him.

He walked towards the door and he could still hear the

music playing, that slow, haunting, jack in the box music. He stopped in front of the door and reached his hand out. He was overcome with stifling fear.

What if he opened the door and the jack in the box sprang to life?

What if he opened it and the *thing* came flying through?

Could the music be some weird countdown, waiting for him to open the door so it could pounce. He shook his head, he had to stop thinking these stupid thoughts, it was just his mind playing tricks on him again. He knew there was no ice cream truck, it was all a figment of his imagination.

He opened the door and walked outside.

"Fuck." He didn't shout, it was like a loud whisper.

The truck was there, that music still playing. It didn't seem right though, the music wasn't loud like an ice cream truck. If he hadn't been sat in silence he wasn't sure he would have heard it at all. The ice cream truck sat there, across the road from him, in the dark, playing that song like a giant music box on wheels.

It can't be real.

He was trying to convince himself. He snuck towards the truck, glancing around to see if anyone was nearby, there didn't seem to be anyone nearby. He was next to it now, his hands were shaking. He reached out and touched it.

"Oh my God, it's real."

He took a step back, it was really there, the music was still playing, the same tune on loop, still that slow haunting music. It was embedded into his head now.

"If . . . you . . . go . . . down . . . to . . . the . . . woods . . . today"

Trembling, Dave moved around to the driver's side and peeked in the window. There was no one to be seen. Where had they gone? Someone had to have been driving this thing, he couldn't believe they would just leave it on the side of the road, music still playing and everything. He looked inside again. It was unlocked, and he knew he shouldn't, but he opened the door.

Something about this just wasn't right.

He had to have a look inside this truck. He pulled himself in, leaning over so his legs were still hanging out the door, he was straining his ears trying to hear if anyone was coming. All he could hear was that awful music. He had to be quick. As he looked around, he couldn't really see anything unusual. It was too dark to see anything properly, the light inside the truck didn't seem to work. Dave was thankful for this, otherwise the owner or this thing would've been able to see the light on from a distance.

"Oh well, weird, fuck it."

Dave jumped out. Okay, so there was a creepy old ice cream truck parked outside in the middle of the night. *It wasn't really important was it?* It was probably just some old guy who forgot to turn the music off and lock the thing up. It was one of the creepiest things he had seen, and he was sure that he would never get that god forsaken *Teddy Bears Picnic* in ultimate slow mode out of his head, but that's all it was, just creepy. He decided that this was probably more down to his frame of mind right now, he had been sitting in the dark for nights on end waiting for some crazed killer to turn up. In his warped, and now fragile, mind, this was probably perfect for the horror story he had been fabricating in his head.

He heard screams.

"Oh shit! That *was* real."

He sprinted across the road and crouched down behind the bushes next to his house. He could still see the ice cream truck from his hiding place.

I knew it, he thought. *That creepy fuckin thing belongs to that crazy bastard, to that thing.*

He heard screams again.

His heart was racing, his hands were trembling, and so he stayed crouched, hidden in the bushes. He needed to see what he was dealing with here. He needed some form of plan; what was he going to do? He had to get whatever that thing was to take him to his mother.

How could he do that? He couldn't just walk up and ask, "Hey, crazy guy, can I have my mother back please?" He decided he was going to have to wait, then when the moment was right, he could follow this freak. He was sure that it would lead him to his captured mother.

Then he could save her, he didn't know how he was going to do it but he knew had to do something.

He stayed crouched, watching the ice cream truck, waiting for the *thing* to appear, the music still playing.

"If . . . you . . . go . . . down . . . to . . . the . . . woods . . . today."

"I really hate that song."

Chapter 15

"What the hell is that?" Dave said to himself.

He looked over into the dim patch of light just past the ice cream truck. He could see the shadow of what looked like a monster, it was huge. As the creature crept into the light he began to see features appear. It wasn't a monster, he didn't think so anyway. The face was still hidden in darkness, there was only a black space where it should be. What Dave could see was this guy was *big*, really big. Must have been at least six-foot-ten and he was wider than any man he had ever seen. It was like looking at a gorilla, a gorilla that was walking upright like a man.

Jesus, it's fuckin' Bigfoot, Dave thought.

The gorilla was carrying something over his shoulder and something else was glistening in his other hand. It might have been a knife or something metal. What was the other thing he was carrying on his shoulder? There was something dangling from either side, like a fireman carrying someone from a burning building. It was a person, it was only small but it was a person. It must have been a child.

The light shone across the small thing's face. It was definitely a child, it was a young boy, must have only been about ten or twelve. *Where the hell was he taking him?* What had he done to him? He must have done something if that other thing in its hand *was* a knife.

Dave remained crouched down and watched the gorilla-like creature carry the boy along like a rag doll. This yeti was walking really slowly and when he reached the truck, he pulled the side window open and flung the boy straight through the side window into the ice cream truck. This guy must have been really strong as it didn't even look like he needed to put any effort into shifting the kid.

He climbed into the truck and reached up for something. The music stopped. The silence fell over Dave like a heavy quilt of fear, he hadn't notice the music was still playing until that moment. He didn't realise that although it had freaked him out before, it was a lot more comforting than this complete silence. Bigfoot walked slowly around the truck, opened the back door and grabbed something from inside. Dave couldn't quite see what it was, but there were two things. It looked like two buckets? The giant slammed the back door shut and then strolled along back into the shadows. He was whistling something. It was a slow whistle as he strolled along.

It was *Teddy Bears Picnic.*

Oh no, not that again, Dave thought. *Change the fucking tune!*

Bigfoot whistling it was even creepier than the music that had been playing before. It was in the same slow and creepy timing and Dave found himself humming along.

"If . . . you . . . go . . . down . . . to . . . the . . . woods . . . today."

Dave tried to shut it out of his mind again, it was freaking him out.

What was in those buckets?

Oh shit. It's the pig blood. Dave realised, his thoughts racing. *If the freak has gone to paint this kid's house with blood then I might have time to get the kid out of that truck.*

He waited for Bigfoot to disappear through the shadows, then began to sneak back out from his hiding spot. He ran over as quietly as he could, reaching for the door that he opened before.

It was locked.

"Dammit!"

How could the bastard forget to lock his door before but then remember to lock it in between going to spread blood everywhere? Maybe he could try the back door. He ran around as fast as he could, not knowing how much time remained before Bigfoot returned. He tried frantically to open the back door, which was locked as well. What could he do? He was running out of time.

"Shit!"

Maybe he could smash the window. Immediately, he looked around for something he could use to break the window to the truck. Then, he heard something.

"You're . . . in . . . for . . . a . . . big . . . surprise."

It was that slow whistling again. Bigfoot was coming back.

Dave spun to run away and slipped as he turned, tumbling to the ground. He banged his head as he landed on the concrete, dazing himself for a second.

He looked up, he could see a giant emerging from the shadows.

"Oh, shit," he cried out in a whisper.

He dragged himself across the street and dived into the bushes. Did Bigfoot see him?

Was it coming to get him?

He was too scared to turn around and look. *What if this freak hadn't seen him but then he made so much noise trying to turn around that he drew attention to himself?* He closed his eyes tight and stayed as still as he could in the bushes. He knew any minute now that Bigfoot's giant paw was going to grab his shoulder and drag him backwards. Dave remembered the thing that guy had been carrying, the knife-like object. This thing was going to drag him out of the bush and the cut him to pieces with that knife.

He waited, this was it: the moment he was going to die.

A sudden bang made him jump.

"What was that?"

It was a door, it was Bigfoot getting into the truck. The engine started, and so did the freaky jack in the box music.

"You'd . . . better . . . believe . . . your . . . eyes."

He was leaving, Bigfoot was leaving. Dave had to do something now or he'd lose his chance. This is what he had been waiting for, this was his chance, and he had to take it.

He climbed out from the bushes to see the ice cream truck pulling slowly out of the street.

Dave ran.

He pushed himself to run as fast as he could, he imagined himself back on the tracks fighting for first place. He could feel the wind rushing passed him again, he could feel his body trembling, the adrenaline rushing through his veins. He was flying. He was back in his youth, no one could run as fast as him. This was his time to shine again.

He wasn't fighting for first place this time, he was fighting for his mother's life.

He was fighting to save that little boy locked in the back of the truck.

He gave more effort than he even knew he had, he pushed with every inch of his capability. He had to concentrate so he didn't over run and go tumbling head over heels.

He was getting closer, he was almost there now. He needed to reach the truck before it pulled out of the estate and got onto the main road. If it got onto them and accelerated then he had no chance of catching it. He put in one last ditch attempt, pushing so hard his face was bright red with exertion, he looked like he was going to explode. He didn't have time to wonder Bigfoot had seen him running behind.

He just had to assume that because he hadn't stopped, he hadn't seen him.

Dave was almost there, he reached out and grabbed the back of the truck. He used the last of his energy to pull himself up. He pulled himself as close as he could get to the back of the truck. He spread his arms and legs wide, gripping on for dear life.

Dave knew that wherever this truck was taking him, that's where he would find his mother.

Now he just needed to hold on.

Chapter 16

The reality of what he was doing began to sink in.

Still gripping to the back of the truck, trying his best not to fall off, thoughts started to rush into Dave's head.

"What the hell am I doing? I shouldn't have done this."

The truck picked up speed now, turned onto one of the main roads. Dave was certain that if he fell off at the speed they were going, the impact would probably kill him. He tightened his grip, as best as he could.

He started creating scenarios in his mind.

What if Bigfoot knew that Dave was hanging on to the back of the truck?

What if he was just waiting until he reached a quiet spot to pull over and then kill him?

Dave hadn't thought this through, he didn't even have any weapons to protect himself. Even if the gorilla didn't use a weapon, one on one, this giant would crush Dave. He would be completely helpless. No, he had to stop thinking this way. He hadn't been seen, surely if the freak had seen him he would've got him before he left and thrown him in the back with that kid.

Oh, shit, the kid, Dave thought.

Was he still alive? He must be, if this freak was going to kill the kid then why would he use the fake blood back at the house? There must be a chance the kid was still alive. He had been unconscious, he definitely wasn't moving when Dave watched the freak throw him into the truck. What if he *was* dead? Dave had been hugging the back of this truck and just on the other side of the door was this kid's dead body?

What if it was all messed up?

Dave started to imagine the kid bleeding, his blood beginning to creep out from under the door, dripping passed Dave's feet, leaving a red trail along the ground.

No, he *had* to stop thinking like this. The kid was alive, he was.

What about his mother? She had been gone for a while, for well over two weeks. There could be a big chance that she was already dead. The police had said the blood in the house didn't belong to her but that didn't mean that she hadn't bled since. What was that freak doing with the people he took? What if he was torturing them or something? Doing all the sick things that the freaks on the movies do, the movies that Dave enjoyed watching so much.

What if he got there and his mum had been cut into little pieces to be fed to the dogs?

Dave's stomach tightened, he had to concentrate hard to stop the vomit from rising up to his throat. If he started puking now he would fall off the back of the truck for sure.

The thought of his mother like that was too much.

He had to think positively. This is what he had been waiting for, wasn't it? This is why he had sat up all those nights looking out of the window. He had been waiting for this freak to turn up, and now he had. He was leading Dave to the place where, hopefully, his mother was being held. This was even better than he'd hoped for.

This freak was going to drive him straight to her.

He could sneak out and get her, then he could go and get the kid and lead them to their escape. He could rescue them. After they were free he would be able to tell the police exactly where this sick bastard was hiding out. The police could go along and arrest him then see if he had any other people held there.

Lisa was still there, Dave thought, *he didn't know how many more.*

But the point was, after the police had gone and arrested the guy, Dave would be the hero. He would have saved the day. He would probably be given a medal of bravery from the police. He would most likely even have his picture in the paper, and be on the news.

The truck started to slow down but Dave couldn't see where they were going with his face pressed to the back.

They must be close, he had to be ready to jump off and hide before Bigfoot came around to grab him.

Chapter 17

The truck slowed almost to a stop.

Dave chose this opportunity to jump off and run behind a group of large red bins. He crouched down and peeked over the top.

Was he seen? It didn't look like it. *Thank God,* he thought.

The ice cream truck crawled forward at a snail's pace, like a customer driving around a red light district looking for a hooker. Eventually it stopped, it was only one building away from where Dave had chosen his hiding space. Dave looked around.

"Where the hell am I?"

He was surrounded by huge, old-looking buildings. They looked like factories of some sort. He could smell something horrible, like sea air mixed with smog and decaying trash. He looked farther down the street, he could see water. He was at the docks. There were huge swaths of industrial land that stretched into the distance, each with old buildings that had been used as factories and warehouses. As far as he knew, they had been abandoned for years.

Dave always wondered why they hadn't been demolished or reconstructed. The recession had affected every area of industry so there was no money to build any businesses up; everything had been left to go to waste. Which was evident by the rows of derelict buildings.

Bigfoot got out of the truck. It was so dark that even at the other end of the street, Dave could still hear the freak whistling that haunting tune.

"If . . . you . . . go . . . down . . . to . . . the . . . woods . . . today."

It strolled to the back of the truck, unlocked the door and threw it open. Dave saw the boy run at the freak, his arms raised in the air, screaming. The giant man didn't even flinch as the boy collided with him, he simply grabbed him with one hand around his throat, lifted him up in the air and slammed the small body back down to the floor of the ice cream truck. The sound the impact made echoed through the streets. Dave began to tremble as he watched the boy's body go limp.

"Oh shit, he's killed him now."

The giant threw the lifeless body over his shoulder and strolled towards the building, still whistling, as though he were plodding along with his nine to five job.

"You're . . . sure . . . of . . . a . . . big . . . surprise."

Dave's view was partially blocked by some more bins and protruding walls farther down the street. He heard a loud bang, like a metal fence being punched. He leaned around the bin to get a better look. The freak had gone. He must have gone through a door in the next building.

Dave's heart began to beat like a hummingbird, he was struggling for air, he tried to calm himself as he began to hyper ventilate. He knew that he was going to have to follow that freak into the building. He had come all this way, he *had* to go and find his mother. He walked slowly and as quietly as he could down the dark street. The street lights were aglow but they were spaced lengths apart and the street was very narrow with tall buildings on either side.

This left a lot of black, shadowy spots on the street. Dave thought he could use these to his advantage, as he crept down the street, and thought if that guy came back out he could hide in the shadow.

He continued his walk, almost holding his breath, waiting for the moment this giant emerged from the darkness, standing over him with a meat cleaver or a chainsaw. He reached the ice cream truck; it had been left in the middle of the road. Dave knew that no one would be coming near this building anytime soon. It was just him, Bigfoot and whoever was being held captive inside. Unless . . . unless Bigfoot had friends inside. Dave hadn't thought about that.

What if he got inside and there was a gang of these crazed killers?

What would he do then? He wouldn't even stand a chance hiding, let alone fighting if there was a group of them.

He stood outside, looking up at the tall abandoned factory, thinking that this would probably be his final act, this would be his final resting place. He could see a sign half way up the front.

Windas Development.

It had a picture of a conservatory next to the writing. It was a window factory that had obviously been left abandoned a long time ago.

For a window factory it had surprisingly few windows, Dave thought.

He could see some farther down the street but they were quite high up. It didn't matter, he *had* to have a look inside before even attempting to go in there. He needed to have some idea of what he was up against.

He ran down the street until he was stood underneath the raised windows, but there was no way he could reach them. He needed something to climb on. He rolled one of the big bins from the side of the road until it was placed under the window. The top of the bin itself was high up, it was just above Dave's shoulder, so getting up on that wasn't the easiest task.

After some effort on his part, he was there, stood upright on the bin. He still had to really stretch himself up to see in the window. It was really dark, it looked like the window had been painted. There were some spots where the paint didn't appear as thick.

Dave cupped his eyes and tried to look in. He couldn't tell if it was dark inside or if it was just the paint on the window making it look that way. He strained to see something inside, to see anything. He couldn't, all he could see was the dark floor.

However, the floor was moving.

There was movement all over the floor, he couldn't see what it was. There were shadows raising and dropping. It looked like a giant carpet that was being shaken from side to side in the dark. There were things in that factory moving around. He didn't know what they were, maybe they were guard dogs? Couldn't be, not that many, and anyway, these things weren't moving like they were walking, these things were squirming along on the floor.

But what *were* they?

And how many of them were there?

Chapter 18

"I need to find a way in," Dave whispered to himself.

The window he had been looking through, apart from being too high up, was locked. He would have to smash it to get through and then it would be at least a ten foot drop, probably face first.

No he didn't want to choose that route.

There had to be another way, there had to be more windows somewhere. Maybe around the back? Dave ran down to the end of the street and then across to the next street behind the building.

"Shit!" he said.

He didn't need to go any farther up to see that the window factory was joined at the back to another building. Probably another old factory, there were definitely no windows at the back.

"There has to be somewhere."

He ran back up the street, passed the factory, ducking and diving in the shadows, stopping every now and then to crouch behind another big red bin. He had to be ready to hide if that freak came back out. When he reached the end of the factory, he noticed that there was a low roof connecting it to the next building. Perhaps it had been an extension added on years ago? Perhaps it was a toilet block or something? It didn't matter what it was, it might have a window or a sky light that he could get through.

He spread his arms and legs to each side and began to shimmy up the narrow walls that were protruding on either side of the low roof. He remembered doing this sort of thing when he was a kid. It had seemed a lot easier back then. After a lot of climbing and a lot of grunting, he reached the top of the roof.

"Yes," he said.

There was a window on the connecting wall of the factory, it wasn't very big, probably only used to let a bit of light into a bathroom or something.

Worth a shot, he thought.

He tiptoed across the roof and knelt down next to the window, he was shrouded by darkness, crouched in the narrow gap on the small roof between the larger buildings. He leant over to try and see into the window; he wanted to see if it would be a safer route than the high one he had been looking in before. As he leaned forward he was stopped about an inch short of the window when something pressed against his forehead.

"Fuck."

There was a metal grate nailed to the outside of the window. He had seen the checked lines when the window first came in sight but he thought it was just a pattern. Looks like this route wasn't going to work either. He snuck back across the low roof and lowered himself down. He tried to drop quietly but the drop was bigger than he anticipated and he made a loud thud. He dropped hard onto his knee, smacking it against the concrete floor.

"Ow . . . shit! *Mother fucker!* That *hurt,*" he cursed

There has to be a way in, there has to be, he thought.

He prowled around the front of the factory once more. There were three large sliding metal doors, but they were bolted with big industrial pad locks; he wasn't getting through them without bolt cutters. He knew there was only one way in, it was the only way he hoped he wouldn't have to go through.

He had to go through the door that Bigfoot had entered earlier.

His thoughts returned to all the different ways that the giant freak was going to kill him. He was going to open the door and that bastard was going to be waiting on the other side with a shotgun. He would blow his brains all over the wall. No, he would open the door and be impaled with a big spear. No it would be an axe to the head. No, he had to stop these thoughts again, he had to be brave, he had to go and save his mother.

His legs were trembling as he shuffled toward the rusty metal door. His hand shook as he reached out for the handle and turned it. The door was unlocked, it creaked as he opened it, he flinched with every movement, each creak seemed like it was as loud as fireworks in the silent, dark night.

Shhh, shut up, shut up, shut up, he thought.

After mere seconds, but what seemed to be a lifetime, the door was open. There was no one there, thank God. He crouched down, hurried through the door and ducked into a dark corner directly ahead of him. The place was lit, but only just. All the lights seemed to be a kind of dull orange colour, the colour of pumpkins on Halloween. They were so filthy that the dirt and dust on them had effectively masked the light.

Dave was faced with two doors, one at the end of the corridor and one to his left. Either side of the door to the left were large windows, overlooking what Dave assumed would be the factory shop floor. He needed to see what it was that had been squirming down there.

He had to check the killer wasn't there before he went storming in.

He crawled to the window and lifted his head just enough so his eyes were peeking over the edge of sill. He still couldn't see properly. He lifted himself more almost to a standing position. It was too dark, that guy couldn't be in there, if he was, he couldn't see anyway and Dave would be able to sneak past in the shadows, hopefully.

"Shit, this is crazy, I'm gonna die," he thought.

He shimmied over until he was directly in from of the door to the shop floor.

He opened it.

Holy shit what is that smell?

Dave gagged.

Chapter 19

Dave covered his mouth and nose with his hand in an attempt to mask the awful smell.

It didn't work, the smell was too strong.

He imagined it crawling through his fingers and creeping into his nostrils. It was the most disgusting thing he'd smelt in his life. He didn't know exactly what a rotting corpse smelled like, but if he had to guess, it would smell like this.

He made his way down the metal staircase leading to the shop floor. He flinched with each movement. Even trying as he was to be quiet, it still rattled when his foot touched the next step. The staircase ended at the far left corner of the room. When Dave reached the bottom he turned and started to walk to the centre of the room.

"Oh my God," he shuddered.

Now that Dave was on the shop floor he could see the things that had been squirming on the floor. They covered almost the entire surface, from wall to wall. He didn't know exactly how many there were but he knew *what* they were.

They were people.

Jesus, how many are there? He wondered. *How long have they been here?*

Dave's stomach turned at the sight of these people. He couldn't see them all, it was too dark, but when he crouched down he could see the ones nearest to him. The first person he looked at was missing an eye. He couldn't tell whether it was a man or woman, the face was too messed up. The bottom lip looked like it had been ripped from the face, the teeth left bare. Only one or two remained, embedded into a jaw that looked dislocated.

Dave put the back of his hand close to the mutilated mouth. There was no air coming out, this person wasn't breathing. *Poor bastard got tortured*, he thought.

He could see that this person's leg was facing the wrong way, the hip must have been broken or dislocated. There was a huge lump on the bottom of the leg. Dave leaned over to see what it was.

"Oh fuck! Holy shit . . . "

It was an arm. The hand had been severed, but Dave could clearly see that there was an arm attached to this other person's leg. It had been sewn on. His eyes followed the arm along past the elbow leading to the shoulder, the arm was still attached to its owner. The face that had been half sewn onto the other arm did not belong.

Dave leaned over and puked. He couldn't hold back anymore. The sight was too horrific.

What type of sick human being could do something like this?

This was worse than the things you see in horror films. He couldn't in his wildest nightmares imagine anyone could do this to other people.

Dave walked slowly along the floor, having to carefully step over various limbs and torsos. The bodies were spread all the way across to the other side, each one sewn onto the next, making one huge patchwork of skin and different body parts.

The further along Dave walked, the more he noticed that the bodies had not started to rot, unlike the ones at the other end of the room. Perhaps the ones closest to the stairs had been there for longer. This freak must have just added bodies onto his sick work of art as and when they came in. Almost like a production line.

Mum, he thought.

If his production line theory was correct, that meant his mother would most likely be at the far end of the factory, and hopefully not in as bad a state as the earlier victims. Dave started to rush toward the end of the factory, careful not to fall over any of the mutilated patchwork victims.

"Help me," he heard a whisper.

Dave stopped.

"Hel . . . help . . . me," he heard again.

When Dave looked down, he could see that the people surrounding him now had definitely not been there for as long as the ones he'd seen prior. There was more colour to their skin, their clothes didn't look quite as bad, and their blood seemed more . . . fresh.

Dave turned away and puked again.

"Help . . . please."

He looked down and saw movement, not from just one person but from several. He could see a face, its lips moving.

"Help me . . . "

He couldn't see exactly where the body was though, there were four or five bodies moving. Obviously *one* of them belonged to this person, but it had been sewn to the others. So when it moved, they all moved.

"It's ok," Dave said in a whisper, "I'm here to help you."

"Help . . . me . . . "

"Yes I'm here to help you, how long have you been here?"

"Please."

"Do you know if there are any more alive?"

"Help . . . "

"Have you seen a woman come in, in the last few weeks?"

" . . . me."

Dave began to get frustrated, this person's mind had left them already, they were completely oblivious to what Dave was saying. They were left with nothing but their survival instinct. To ask for help.

"Please help me . . . ," the face attached to multiple bodies said again.

"I promise you, I'm going to try . . . but."

The lights turned on.

Chapter 20

"If . . . you . . . go . . . down . . . to . . . the . . . woods . . . today"

It was the whistling again.

Bigfoot was coming!

Dave needed to find a place to hide and fast. His eyes shot in every direction, there were plenty of things he could hide behind. Machinery, old unused PVC doors, a big furnace and a kiln. He couldn't get to any of these things fast enough though, the door at the top of the stairs opened.

Dave dropped to the floor.

Keeping himself as still as possible, he used just his feet to push him into the human patchwork quilt. He tucked his chin to his chest so his head was pressed against the floor and then pushed his body forwards, further and further, until eventually he was covered by the bodies. To anyone looking from the outside they would not notice him, he was underneath parts of five different bodies, all sewn together to camouflage him.

"You're . . . in . . . for . . . a . . . big . . . surprise."

The whistling was getting louder. Dave could hear the footsteps of the maniac. He was coming down the stairs.

". . . if . . . you . . . go . . . down . . . "

He had reached the bottom of the stairs.

" . . . to . . . the . . . woods . . . "

He was close, Dave could hear the steps and the whistling getting louder and louder the closer he got.

" . . . today . . . you'd . . . "

Dave lay as still as the corpses he was surrounded by.

He knew now that this mad man was stood right next to him.

Can he see me? Dave thought.

He held his breath and kept his chin tucked right into his chest, trying his best not to make a sound, trying his best not to move. He braced himself, waiting for the freak to strike. He knew any minute now that this freak was going to grab him and drag him out from underneath the quilt of bodies he was covered by.

"Better . . . go . . . in . . . disguise."

It was moving away, the whistling was moving! Dave had gone unnoticed.

Thank God, he thought.

He let out a breath, as slow and as quietly as he could. He wanted desperately to turn around so he could see where Bigfoot was. He knew that the freak had continued through the factory but he couldn't see what he was doing or where he was. The anticipation was killing him.

". . . for . . . every . . . bear . . . that . . . ever . . . there . . . was."

Dave heard a strange noise, metal sliding against something, like the noise they make on martial arts films when the samurai removes his sword from its sheath.

Oh shit, he's got a knife now, Dave thought. *He did see me, he just went to get a weapon, now he's gonna come back and get me.*

Dave's heart started racing, the fear was consuming him. This freak was going to come and kill him now and he was just going to lie there and wait for it to happen.

This is it, this is how I'm going to die, hiding under a pile of dead bodies.

"No, no, no, no, please, please *nooooooo*!" A woman screamed.

Dave breathed a sigh of relief.

His immediate thought following this was that he was a horrible person, feeling relieved to know that the freak had killed someone else instead. He couldn't help it though, he had been given another chance and he was happy; he wasn't ready to die.

"Would . . . gather . . . there . . . for . . . certain."

The freak continued to whistle as he dragged the poor woman away.

"*Noooo, help!*" She screamed.

The screaming was followed by a loud thud, which was followed by silence.

Dave waited a moment.

"Because . . . today's . . . "

The whistling was back.

" . . . The . . . day . . . the . . . teddy . . . bears . . . have . . . their . . . picnic."

Dave continued to lie still, listening to the whistling pass him and slowly disappear up the stairs. He heard the door shut. The lights were turned off again. Dave shuffled and slid his way out from under his hiding spot beneath the bodies. He stayed sat for a moment and leaned against the wall. He took deep exaggerated breaths in and out like he had been deprived of oxygen for the past ten minutes. Eventually he regained his composure. From his sitting position he turned and looked to the door at the top of the stairs.

"That other door in the corridor," he said to himself,

"that's where he's taken that woman. That must be the place he takes his victims to torture them."

This thought shook Dave's stomach again. He quickly stood up, remembering his grotesque surroundings.

"I've got to figure out a way to stop him."

Dave marched towards the rear end of the factory, he was getting to the more 'fresh meat' of the production line now. Not all of these bodies were hacked up and sewn back together yet. Some of these had just been tied up. Some were conscious, some were not. All looked to be in a world of their own. They had gone somewhere in their mind to escape this hell they had found themselves in.

Dave scanned over the newer victims. He still couldn't see his mother. He didn't have time to go through each and every one of them.

I've got to stop him, he thought again. I've got to stop him before he hurts another person, before he gets to mum." His voice broke as he began to cry.

He straightened himself up, took a deep breath.

There must be something around here I can use as a weapon.

Chapter 21

Dave couldn't believe his luck.

He had marched to the rear end of the factory in search of something he could use as a weapon. In search of *anything* he could use as a weapon. What he found was a *pile* of weapons. All lay in heaps on the floor next to each other were knives—lots of knives –, a pick axe, a chainsaw, a wood cutting axe, something which looked like a spear, chains, metal bars, and hammers.

If this had been a computer game, Dave would have found a secret room to come across all these weapons.

He stood staring down at the pile in amazement. He couldn't believe that Bigfoot had just left all this here. Surely any one of these victims scattered around could grab one of these weapons to use against their captor. Dave turned around to look at the never-ending array of bodies on the floor.

No, he sighed, *none of these people would have been able to get anywhere near these weapons.* They were all either too badly mutilated or were bound and gagged. It must have been like a tease to them. Lying on the floor looking at all these tools and weapons, just wishing that they were able to get their hands on one of them to defend themselves.

That thought must have undoubtedly been followed by the horrific thought in which they realised that these things were going to be used on *them.*

"Cruel bastard," Dave said to himself. "He left the weapons here to taunt them."

Dave could see lots of eyes had fallen upon him. Pupils

staring at him from all directions on the floor.

Those eyes were talking to him.

Help us.

They didn't need words, he could see it. They all looked at him in hope. Helpless people looking to him to save them. He knew that even if he tried to untie and free them one by one, the ones that were still alive at least, they wouldn't get far. There was definitely no chance that he would be able to save anywhere near enough of them, let alone all of them.

No, he had decided what he needed to do.

The only way to save these people was to kill that crazy freak that brought them here. And now he had the weapons to do it. Thanks to the laziness and cocky attitude of this sick bastard, he had left everything that Dave would need to take him down.

Dave looked down at the weapons again. He had images in his head of him being tooled up like some super soldier, with knives and axes and spears all tucked in different compartments of some cool outfit. With weapons all hung in perfectly co-ordinated places so he could grab the exact one he wanted when he wanted.

Back to reality though, he didn't have some cool outfit, or the body of a superhero. These things were heavy and there is no chance he could take them all. He wouldn't be able to carry much, and what he did carry would weigh him down.

His weapon of choice was to be the axe, apart from the fact he decided it was possibly the coolest weapon there, he also thought that if he could get a good swing it would probably do the most damage. This guy he was going up against was huge, he needed a high impact weapon to use against him. "Axe it is then," he said to himself, trying to build confidence.

Dave grabbed the axe and began his march to the stairs, leaving all the other tools and weapons behind.

He ascended the stairs, his legs began to tremble once more, he felt bile coming up from his stomach again.

No, come on Dave, he thought, *you have to do this, for mum. You can't be scared now.*

But he was scared, he didn't think it was possible to be any more scared that he felt right now. He opened the door to the corridor. It was still lit by the dim orange light he had seen earlier. With the axe ready in his hand he approached the next door at the end of the corridor. He held the axe above his head with his right hand, ready to strike when needed, and he opened the door with his left hand.

It was another corridor. He entered, he could hear screaming now.

"Bastard must be busy," he said.

He began to move towards the sound of the screams, they got louder as he moved closer. He came to the end of the corridor where he was faced with a door that had *office* embossed onto it. There was a pane of glass on the door but it was patterned so Dave couldn't see through it properly. He could see something moving behind it, but he couldn't make out what it was.

"*Arghhhhhh.*" He heard a scream again.

That scream was really loud, they must be right on the other side of this door, he thought. He stood ready with the axe propped in both hands, waiting for his moment.

Ok, Dave, this is it, he thought, *there's no turning back now, you've come this far.*

Sweat was dripping from his head.

You have to do this, you have to save mum, and those people.

His hands had become clammy, he had to twist them on the shaft of the axe to improve his grip. *Come on Dave, this is it, you can do it.* His heart was racing, his stomach felt like it was doing somersaults.

Just run in there and put this axe through that bastard's head.

He braced himself.

Ok, come on, come on. He took a deep breath.

He leaned back and kicked the door open.

Chapter 22

"*Arghhhh,*" Dave screamed.

He rushed into the office with the axe raised above his head swinging it from side to side. The freak spun around in shock to see Dave running towards him looking like a maniac.

Dave swung the axe back up ready to strike; the weight of the axe shifted Dave's shoulders to the right, while his feet went left. He slipped on a pool of blood that had leaked onto the floor from Bigfoot's latest victim. Dave toppled over, landing hard on his shoulder, letting out a big grunt when he struck the ground.

The giant began to walk towards him. Dave stared up at the looming monster looking down on him. He managed to lift himself to one knee and swing the axe across to the left.

He got him. He struck the giant freak in the thigh with the axe.

Dave tried to pull it back so he could swing again but it was stuck. It was really difficult to pull it free from the freaks leg. He began yanking back and forth in a panic trying to free the blade. His eyes wide, Dave looked up at the giant that appeared to be un-phased by his new injury.

He just stood staring at Dave with a confused look on his face.

Slowly, he raised his arm above his head. A giant hand came thundering down smacking Dave on the head like a sledge hammer. Dave's head fell flat to the floor like a rock. He let go of the axe, and as if by magic, the axe just simply fell from his opponent's leg when he loosened his grip. Dave pushed both hands on the floor in an attempt to lift himself up. He was hit by another huge blow with knocked him back down.

He tried to push himself up again, he felt a flash of pain to the side of his face. He put his hand to his cheek, he could feel blooding pouring through his fingers. Dave looked up to see Bigfoot stood over him with a knife in his hand.

"Oh, shit . . . "

He tracked backwards in a sitting position, pushing his feet against the floor to move himself, trying to create a bit of space between him and the giant. He stopped when he reached the wall. With his back pressed against the wall, Dave rose to his feet.

He could see a woman on the other side of the room, her hands bound above her head. She was red, completely red. She had literally been bled from head to toe. There was a lump on the floor next to her which Dave assumed to be her scalp, hair attached, as she was left with none on her head. One of her breasts was pumping out blood continuously like a fountain. It was split clean in two, leaving two large flaps of skin hanging either side from each other. Beneath her sliced breast were several wounds and puncture marks from the point in which Bigfoot's knife had entered her stomach. Her body was dangling from the wall. It looked like she was stood up but she wasn't. It was the restraints on her arms holding her up. Luckily for her, she had passed now. Her torture was over.

Dave's hadn't begun yet.

He looked around frantically trying to find something, anything to use to defend himself. There were tools placed around the feet of the poor victim on the other side of the room, but the giant stood between him and them.

No choice, he thought.

Dave made a run for them, he was hit hard, knocking him back down on the floor before he could get anywhere near them. His head was pounding, his vision was beginning to blur. He could see Bigfoot closing in on him.

He tried to get back to his feet.

Before he had chance to stand up again, he could feel himself being lifted. Now, he could feel wind rushing past his face, his arms and legs dangling beneath him, as if he was flying. Then came the impact of the adjacent wall. The giant had thrown him across the room. Dave managed to muster enough energy to raise his head enough to see his opponent close in on him again. He felt the flying sensation again, followed by the impact of the second wall along with incredible pain.

He tried to push his hands on the floor to lift himself up but they did nothing. They just slid beneath him in the pool of blood which now contained Dave's blood as well as the blood from the unfortunate woman hung on the wall.

"Bmmstard," Dave mumbled through his swollen mouth.

The blood oozed from his cheeks, his face was swelling up to be twice the size it had been. He opened his eye to see a boot coming fast to his face.

Darkness followed.

Chapter 23

Dave opened his eyes, he couldn't see anything.

His vision was blurred, just specks of lights flashed here and there. He could feel that his arms were tied up against something. He tried to move them, and he couldn't.

"Help!" he tried to shout.

What came out was a sort of muffled mumble. Something was covering his mouth. He blinked repeatedly and shook his head until his vision eventually became clear. He looked at his arms, they had leather straps tied around them. The straps were fitted to the walls. He tried to shout again but nothing followed apart from the muffled sound he'd made earlier. His eyes shot in every direction, frantically trying to find some way out or something to help him. He looked down, he was stood in a pool of blood.

Oh no, he thought, that's my blood, I'm dying.

There was something next to his foot, a lump of some sort. He moved it with his foot, it was hair. He recognised it from before, it was that woman's hair. He had taken that woman's place strapped to the wall. He remembered her wounds, he remembered what the freak had done to her. Scalped her, cut her to ribbons.

Oh, God, no, his thoughts racing, *please, please, please, God no!*

"Mmmphhhh!" his cries for help were still muffled.

He could hear something.

It was whistling.

". . . if . . . you . . . go . . . down . . . to . . . the . . . woods . . . today."

The giant was returning. He tugged his arms back and forth trying to free them from their restraints. He couldn't loosen the grip on the leather straps. Tears flooded across his cheeks.

Oh, God, I'm gonna die, he thought.

The door opened. The freak walked in. Dave tried to shout some form of insult or obscenity at the giant but nothing apart from mumbles left his covered lips. The giant bald killer walked at a slow pace towards Dave, you could almost call it strolling. He stopped right in front of Dave. His eyes, giant pools of darkness, stared into Dave's eyes. Dave had to blink to clear his vision, it had become blurred again from his eyes filling with tears.

The freak, still gazing into Dave's eyes, tilted his head. The way a dog would when it was confused by his master's call. That gaze seemed to last forever. Dave felt as if this freaks huge dark eyes were staring into his soul.

The giant turned around, he was stood staring down at something. Dave struggled to see past the frame of the giant's body. He was looking down at something on a table that had been placed in the room. Dave could see just to the side of the freak. There was a knife on the table, a long, menacing blade with jagged edges. Like a long thin saw. The freak slid it across the table, next to it he placed a cleaver. Then next to that he placed a machete.

Then another knife, then another knife, then another.

"Mmmpphhh! Mmmmpphh" Dave muffled words failed to leave his mouth once more.

I'm gonna die, he thought, *I'm gonna die on this spot.*

The giant slid his index finger back and forth along the

table, pointing it at each blade as he passed it, looking like he was playing a game for which one to choose.

Oh, shit, Dave thought, *eenie, meenie, miney, mo.*

The finger stopped. It looked like the meat cleaver had been this torture sessions weapon of choice. After a slow turn, the freak stood facing Dave once more. He moved close towards him, his eyes forever gazing into Dave's, almost looking lost, looking to Dave for an answer.

What do you want? Dave screamed in his mind.

The freak tilted his head again, what crazy thoughts were passing through his mind? What could he be possibly contemplating at this point?

Never losing eye contact with Dave, Bigfoot's arm swung up and then flew back down so fast that if you blinked you would have missed it. He looked away from Dave's eyes at something on the wall. Then his gaze returned back to Dave's face. Dave looked at the monster, confused, he could feel something trickling down his arm. He looked up.

Oh shit, my hand . . .

The freak had chopped Dave's hand off with one clean swipe of his blade. Dave's arm, no longer being held by the leather strap, dropped to his side. Dave lifted it to his face, looking at the bloody stump that used to hold his hand.

Tears streamed down his face, adrenaline kept him standing, he cried to scream but nothing came out. He swung his arm at the freak, his stump leaving red marks on Bigfoot's shoulder and chest each time it made impact. With each pathetic attempt to inflict some form of pain on the freak, Dave received nothing in return, except a confused look.

The freak dropped the cleaver on the spot where he was stood. He didn't even look down to see it hit the ground. He turned around and made his slow exit back out of the small office room. The door closed behind him.

Dave could hear the whistling getting more faint as the giant got further away.

". . . if . . . you . . . go . . . down . . . to . . . the . . . woods . . . today."

Chapter 24

Holding his bloody stump up to his face, Dave stared in disbelief, tears pouring down his face like the blood pouring from the gaping wound at the end of his arm.

I have to get out of here, he thought.

He looked down to the floor and stared at his abandoned hand. Ironically, the cleaver that had taken the hand had landed next to it, leaving them lying together, side by side. Dave looked up at his other arm, still strapped to the wall.

I need to get that arm free, I need to get out.

With his other arm free from restraint, Dave was now able to turn his body around so he could face the wall. He reached his bloody stump up to the arm held against the wall. The leather strap had a loose bit hanging down. If Dave could push that strap against the wall, maybe he could loosen it.

Maybe he could free his other arm.

With excruciating pain shooting through his whole body, Dave used his stump to push the strap against the wall. He blood streamed down the wall like a fresh tin of paint had been thrown at it. He twisted and wriggled his arm, still holding the strap still with his stump—he could feel the leather begin to loosen on his wrist.

"It's working, it's working."

With the pain almost unbearable and sweat drenching his face, he gritted his teeth and continued to wriggle his hand. He twisted, he tucked his thumb, his index finger and his little finger in to the centre of his hand. He twisted and pulled his hand down. The strap under the stump slid up the wall a bit, sending a stabbing pain right up the side of Dave's body. Pushing through the pain, Dave pushed his stump harder against the wall. He tugged his other hand down.

It came free.

I did it, he thought.

He stood for a second, amazed at what he had just accomplished, his senses returning. He grabbed the thing covering his mouth. His was some sort of tape. He ripped it off, he was sure that in other circumstances tearing that tape off may have been extremely painful, but in light of his recent injuries, he didn't feel anything.

"Ok, what now?" Dave said to himself. "If you get free, he would expect you to run."

With hundreds of thoughts racing through his head, he couldn't decide what to do. He knew one thing though. He couldn't run. He wouldn't get far enough without that freak coming back for him.

Dave hurried to the pool of blood on the floor and grabbed the cleaver. He left the hand behind.

He walked back towards the door and placed his ear to it. There was no one there.

He slowly opened it.

Still no one, he shuffled out of the door. He could see the light to the factory shop floor was on.

"That bastard is down with the bodies, I need to hide."

Dave hurried to the next door in the corridor and let himself in. It was pitch black but that didn't matter, he didn't intend to stay there for long. He closed the door and waited.

Dave must have been waiting for about five minutes. He was still losing a lot of blood and he was sure that if he didn't stop the bleeding soon that he would pass out.

He might bleed to death.

A horrible thought ran through his mind—had he dripped blood along the path to this room? Leading a trail to his demise. No, he knew he hadn't, he had his stump tucked into his stomach, he had looked outside just before entering this room. He definitely hadn't left any trail behind.

Had he?

He could hear the whistling returning.

". . . if . . . you . . . go . . . down . . . to . . . the . . . woods . . . today."

It was the freak coming back, he heard the giant open a door. The whistling stopped, it was followed by an enormous roar.

Dave's host had just discovered that he was missing.

Chapter 25

The giant was raging. He had thrown the table across the room, sending the weapons that had been there scattering along the floor. He punched the wall repeatedly leaving red bloody marks from his fists in a pattern across it. He leaned over propping himself up against the wall, he appeared to be looking down at the hand on the floor. He reached down the pick it up.

To retrieve the one piece of Dave that had been left behind.

He grabbed the hand. As he raised himself back up, Dave jumped onto his back. He felt a sharp pain in his neck.

"*Arghhh!*" Dave screamed "You bastard! You sick, sick *bastard*."

Dave reached around the giant's neck, holding himself on by hooking his stumped arm around it. In his other hand was the meat cleaver that had taken his hand. He swung it over and over again into the giant's neck and shoulder

"Die! You bastard! *Die, die, die.*"

Over and over again, Dave kept swinging the blade into the giant's flesh. Blood was firing out of the freak like a geyser, showering Dave in sheets of red.

The giant wasn't dropping though.

Dave had been cutting him with the cleaver for what seemed like forever. *Why wouldn't he die? Why wouldn't he stop?*

Dave still hooked onto the giants back like a monkey clinging to his mother. Dave kept his stumped arm held tight around the giant's neck. The freak spun back and forth, reaching his arms back in what appeared to be an attempt to get Dave off. The strength seemed to have faded away from him. The freaks hands just stroked against Dave's arms and shoulder. Still Dave continued to thrust the cleaver back and forth into this giant's neck.

After what seemed like an eternity, he dropped to the floor. Dave stood over him, covered from head to toe in blood. The room had been painted red, nowhere appeared to be untouched from the stark crimson. Dave looked to the monster lying on the floor. He climbed onto his back and continued to hack away.

The giant was probably long dead before Dave finally stopped.

He sat on the floor with his back propped against the wall, panting for breath.

"It's over," he sighed.

Chapter 26

Stumbling from side to side, Dave made his way down the corridor, he was beginning to feel faint. He was still bleeding heavily from his arm. He knew that if he didn't stop it soon that he was going to die.

"There must be something around here," he said to himself. "Some rope or something to stop this bleeding."

He managed to carry himself across the corridor and through the door leading to the factory shop floor. He almost fell down the stairs, slipping down several at a time. He eventually reached the bottom and slumped over as he looked across the factory, at the sea of bodies that we placed before him.

"Need to find something . . . " he mumbled.

He made his way to the rear end of the factory, perhaps now he could start thinking about saving some people. He had more time, if he could stop the bleeding. He looked up. There in front of him, he didn't know whether he was happy to see it or horrified. There in front of him stood the kiln, or furnace, or whatever they called it. Some big thing that had once upon a time been used to melt glass and heat metal. He imagined that recently it had only been used to heat torture devices.

"It's lit," he quivered.

Dave knew what he had to do, it was simple. If he didn't stop the bleeding, he was going to die. He took the big tongs that had been leaning against the kiln. Using the tongs, he picked up the largest blade from the pile of weapons that were still scattered on the floor. He held the blade into the flames.

After a long time of waiting, panting for breath, trying to keep the tongs held upright while losing strength in his one good arm, he could see the metal inside the fire begin to glow. He removed the blade from the fire. He dropped the blade to the floor and leaned down. He took deep breaths over and over again.

"Okay, here we go," he said, his voice trembling.

He pressed his stump against the scorching hot blade, cauterising the wound on his arm.

He passed out.

Chapter 27

Dave woke up.

His eyes wide open, he gazed up to the high sheet metal ceiling above him. He could see dim lights hanging from wooden beams placed along the walls. He could smell something burning. It was like a bbq smell, all flesh and charcoal. Not quite as nice though. It reminded him of the smell of burning ants when he was younger. When he would use a magnifying glass to fry them on the pavement. He was lying on a hard concrete floor. Underneath the smell of burnt ants he could smell something else. It was a foul smell, like rotting meat.

He remembered where he was.

He tried to push himself up from the floor. Intense pain shot through him like he had just been struck by lightning. He looked at his arm and saw his stump. The skin now burned and black, flecks of dark blood dried around it. He looked to the floor to see the blade he had used to cauterise it. He could see pieces of his skin that had stuck to it during the horrifically painful process. He used his good arm and leaning to one side, managed to get himself up off the floor.

"Mum," he said to himself. "I need to find Mum."

He began his mission.

He marched up and down the horrific patchwork of bodies. Looked at mangled arms and twisted legs, trying to see if any of them were connected to his mother. He tried to see if he could pick out her face. All the faces he *could* see were so bruised and battered that there would be no way to recognise their owner. He looked for what seemed like for-ever, in fact it was probably about ten minutes.

As he got further down the line he could see the dam-age to these people wasn't quite as bad as the others.

I've got to get help, he thought.

He ran back up the stairs, through the door and down the corridor through the exit of the factory. It was daylight now. He had no idea how long he had been there. He had passed out twice to his knowledge, for all he knows it could have been a couple of hours, it could have been a whole day. That didn't matter, he needed to find a phone. Dave ran up the street from the factory until he reached what looked like a main road. He must have run for fifteen min-utes before he eventually found a payphone at the side of the road. He picked up the phone, he managed to tuck it in between his cheek and his shoulder to hold it in place, and he used his only hand and dialled for the emergency services.

"Police!"

He waited, after a few moments he was connected.

"I'm at a payphone on Glover Street, there is a factory down the road. Windas Development. There are over a hundred bodies there. Some dead, some not."

Dave didn't wait for any reply, he dropped the received and sprinted back to the factory.

"Got to find mum!"

Dave remembered his thought about the production line in the factory earlier. How the people who were more like fresh meat where closer to the rear end of the factory. The long dead bodies were closer to the stairs. Surely his mother had to be closer to the 'fresh' end.

He marched straight down the factory, ignoring all the chopped up and mangled bodies that had been sewn back together. He tried to ignore the helpless gazes of the victims who were still conscious. He had every intention of helping them, but he *had* to find his mother.

He searched for a while. He decided to start untying people as he moved. Some of them were so far beyond recognition that it was the only way he could keep and check on the ones he had already seen. The police stormed through the door just as Dave tore the tape from another victim's mouth. Dave turned around to see the rush of police officers rushing through the corridor and down the stairs.

"Dave?" he heard.

He turned around to see that he had his mother in his arms. He pulled her into his chest and hugged her. He held her close and cried.

"I've found you, Mum, it'll be ok now."

"Dave?" he received a confused reply.

"Don't worry, Mum. It's all over."

Chapter 28

Police officers went in and out of the building. Some of them running out to throw up on the pavement outside. Some came out slowly, shaking their heads.

Dave sat on the pavement outside with his arm held around his mother while waiting for the ambulance that was going to take them to the hospital. Several had been and gone, several more needed to come before all casualties were dealt with.

Dave watched curiously as the officers entered the building then exited it so fast.

Why did they go in there if they can't handle it? They were told what it was like, he saw their colleagues telling them. Was it a job they didn't want to do but had to anyway so put on a brave face and walked in? Was it morbid curiosity? They wanted to see just how bad it was, the patchwork of bodies.

Eventually, Dave's ambulance arrived, he and his mum shared their escort as they were taken to the hospital. He left the police officers to deal with the hell he had just come from.

According to the police, the news reporters, the gossipers, the nurses with loose tones, the doctors with loud voices, this was one of the worst things that had ever been witnessed in this country. Dave heard the conversations go, there had been over two-hundred bodies, over a hundred of them dead. All the dead had been sewn together, all containing different body parts that belonged to different people.

This freak had made his own patchwork quilt, he had

taken off bits and pieces from people and added bits and pieces from other bodies. A vison of hell itself.

Dave spent a very long time in hospital, he had to get numerous treatments and injections for his arm. He had other injuries he either hadn't noticed or had forgotten about that needed treating, like the gaping wound in his cheek from the first round of his fight with Bigfoot. His mother, although not in quite as bad shape as Dave, had been affected a lot more, mentally. She seemed to have left the vessel that was holding her, her mind had drifted somewhere else. Maybe somewhere that she would be able to cope with the sights she had seen. It was going to be a long arduous ordeal Dave was told, psychologically, his mum's brain had been shattered.

It would take years before he got her back, *if* he ever did get her back. This had made Dave cry, all the years he had abused his mother and taken her for granted rushed into his mind. He had flashing images on the times he insulted her, the times he had smashed the place up and she would cower in fear. Now that he realised how horrible and selfish he had been all these years, it might be too late. Now that he wanted to give back to his mother all the love and care that she deserved.

She might be gone. He would be alone.

Chapter 29

One question continued to enter Dave's mind. No matter how many times he tried, he just couldn't answer it.

Why?

Why had that horrible man done all those things?

Was he abused when he was younger? Was he mentally ill? Dave had no doubt that the giant had some form of mental problem, he could see that every time he pictured those big black eyes. Behind those eyes was nothing but an empty void. It was obvious the killer didn't have a very high intellect either. Using pig blood to try and lead the police on a false trail. Didn't he even know about DNA testing & crime scene investigations?

It didn't matter now anyway.

There were no thoughts, no hopes, no dreams. Just darkness.

Perhaps there didn't need to be a reason for it all. Maybe that guy was just evil. Simple as that, he was just evil and wanted people to suffer. He certainly made sure they suffered as much as possible before putting them out of their misery.

It didn't matter, no one could ask him why? That chance had passed, he was gone now. Dave had made sure of that.

Dave was shocked at the amount of thank you cards he received. He also received boxes of chocolate, flowers. People would come to visit him in hospital showering him with hugs and tears of joy and gratitude. These were the family and friends of the survivors. The people that Dave had saved.

In total he was told that seventy-eight people got out of that factory alive. Although some died shortly after, and some had injuries that were beyond help. He had been assured that fifty-six of these people were going to be okay. They were going to live and hopefully, after this, get their lives back. Out of the two hundred and odd that had been held in the factory, fifty-six didn't seem like a huge amount. But everyone kept reminding Dave that without him *none* of them would have survived. And the body count was likely to be a lot more than it was.

It made Dave happy to think about the survivors, to think that they would hopefully get their lives back again, they were given a second chance. So was he, he had to take this chance and use it.

It was time to start appreciating life.

Chapter 30

A year had passed since that horrendous ordeal at the factory. Dave's mum had still not returned home, she was undergoing psychiatric help in the hospital. Still, Dave made sure he had the house spotless. Every day he cleaned from top to bottom and put fresh flowers on the table. Just in case that was the day his mother returned home.

He visited her every day at the hospital. Some days, he wasn't sure that she knew he was there but he went anyway. He would take her a nice bunch of flowers and they would sit together. She would sit silent, Dave didn't know whether she was listening or not, but regardless, he would talk to her for hours. He would tell her about the job he had now, it wasn't much. He struggled to do certain things as he was still getting used to only using one hand. But he had a job at the local shop. Just helping out here and there, helping stack shelves one day or work the till the next day. He didn't get much pay but it was enough and he was happy to be helping the elderly couple that ran the little shop.

He told her about the volunteer work he had been doing, he had been going to the local track and giving tips to new upcoming runners. The coach said that there would be a new assistant's position coming up soon and that Dave was more than welcome to it.

"Hey, I saw Claire as well! Remember Claire?" he said.

Claire had been at the local track while Dave was volunteering. She had a little boy now. She had been weary when she first saw Dave but that faded fast when she saw how he had changed. He was genuinely happy for her. Congratulated her on the wedding and then asked what her son's name was. His name was Phil, he was trying out for the team.

"Wow, he's fast," Dave said, "I'm telling you, with the right training and enough dedication, that kid's gonna be running in the Olympics."

THANK YOU FOR READING

Dear reader, if you have reached this point then hopefully you have enjoyed this book. Firstly I would like to thank you for giving me a chance to entertain you with my story. I know sometimes it is a leap of faith trying an author you have never heard of. Hopefully, as long as people want to read my stories, I can continue to put more out there.

If you did enjoy this story. Would you please consider rating it and leaving a review on sites such as Amazon, Goodreads or any other similar sites? Reviews really do have a huge impact in the self-publishing market. It is the biggest selling tool that we have. Anything you have to say, whether a positive review or some constructive criticism will always be taken on board and used to hopefully improve on future work. Thank you very much. It really does go a long way.

If you would like to see any information regarding my other books you can find details at www.andrewlennon.co.uk

Please also feel free to contact me on Facebook or Twitter I would love to hear your thoughts and feedback.

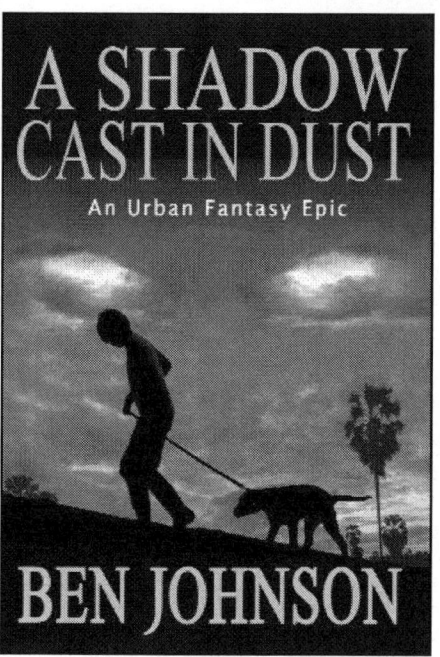

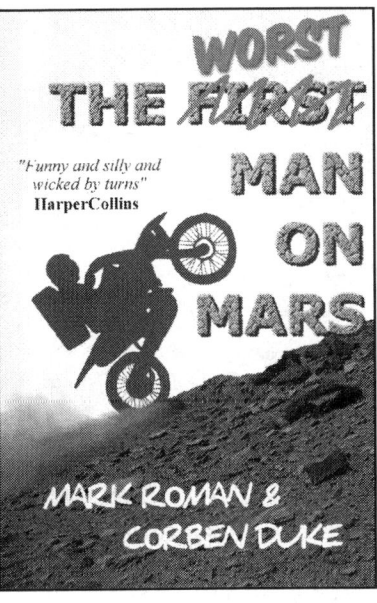

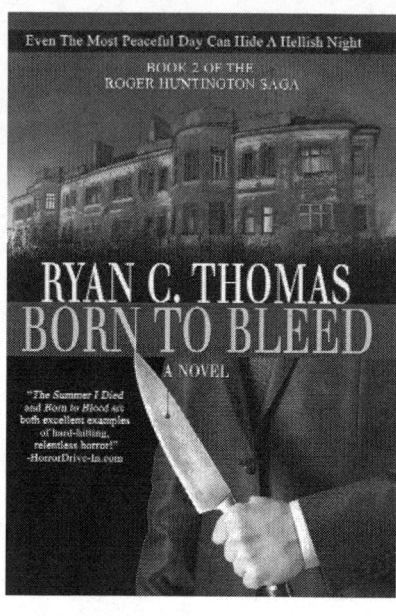
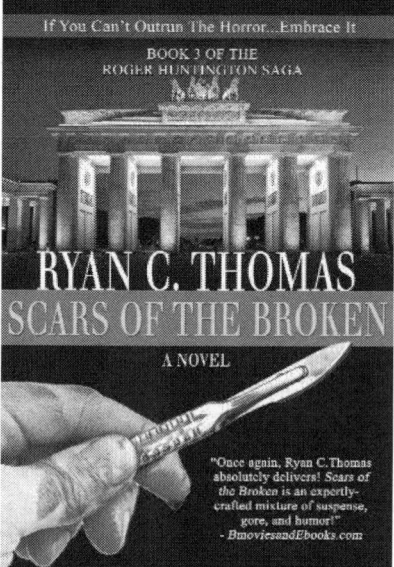

**For more Grand Mal Press titles
please visit us online at
www.grandmalpress.com**

Word of mouth is crucial for any author to succeed. If you enjoyed this book, please consider leaving a review on Amazon or Goodreads. Even a couple sentences can make a world of difference and is very much appreciated. Thank you for reading!

Made in the USA
Charleston, SC
05 December 2016